MW00523183

Rodgers & Hammerstein's

Carousel

Music by
Richard Rodgers

Book & Lyrics by
Oscar Hammerstein II

Based on Ferenc Molnar's play *Liliom*
as adapted by Benjamin F. Glazer

Original Choreography by Agnes de Mille

concord
theatricals

ISBN 978-0-573-70925-8

www.concordtheatricals.com
www.concordtheatricals.co.uk

FOR PRODUCTION INQUIRIES

UNITED STATES AND CANADA
info@concordtheatricals.com
1-866-979-0447

UNITED KINGDOM AND EUROPE
licensing@concordtheatricals.co.uk
020-7054-7298

Each title is subject to availability from Concord Theatricals Corp., depending upon country of performance. Please be aware that *CAROUSEL* may not be licensed by Concord Theatricals Corp. in your territory. Professional and amateur producers should contact the nearest Concord Theatricals Corp. office or licensing partner to verify availability.

MUSIC AND THIRD-PARTY MATERIALS USE NOTE

IMPORTANT BILLING AND CREDIT REQUIREMENTS

CAROUSEL was first produced by the The Theatre Guild at the Majestic Theatre in New York, New York on April 19, 1945. The performance was directed by Rouben Mamoulian, with choreography by Agnes de Mille, orchestrations by Don Walker, dance arrangements by Trude Trittman, musical direction by Joseph Littau, sets by Jo Mielziner, and costumes by Miles White. The production was under the supervision of Theresa Helburn and Lawrence Langer. The cast was as follows:

CARRIE PIPPERIDGE	Jean Darling
JULIE JORDAN	Jan Clayton
MRS. MULLIN	Jean Castro
BILLY BIGELOW	John Raitt
BESSIE	Mimi Strongin
JESSIE	Jimsie Somers
JUGGLER	Lew Foldes
1ST POLICEMAN	Robert Byrn
DAVID BASCOMBE	Franklyn Fox
NETTIE FOWLER	Christine Johnson
JUNE GIRL	Pearl Lang
ENOCH SNOW	Eric Mattson
JIGGER CRAIGIN	Murvyn Vye
HANNAH	Annabelle Lyon
BOATSWAIN	Peter Birch
ARMINY	Connie Baxter
PENNY	Marilyn Merkt
JENNIE	Joan Keenan
VIRGINIA	Ginna Moise
SUSAN	Suzanne Tafel
JONATHAN	Richard H. Gordon
2ND POLICEMAN	Larry Evers
CAPTAIN	Blaker Ritter
1ST HEAVENLY FRIEND	Jay Velie
2ND HEAVENLY FRIEND	Tom McDuffie
STARKEEPER	Russell Collins
LOUISE	Bambi Linn
CARNIVAL BOY	Robert Pagent
ENOCH SNOW, JR.	Ralph Linn
PRINCIPAL	Lester Freedman
SINGERS	Martha Carver,

Iva Withers, Anne Calvert, Connie Baxter, Glory Wills, Josephine Collins, Marilyn Merkt, Joan Keenan, Ginna Moise, Beatrice Miller,

Suzanne Tafel, Verlyn Webb; Joseph Bell, Robert Byrn, Tom Duffey, Blake Ritter, Charles Leighton, Louis Freed, Neil Chirico, Lester Freedman, Richard H. Gordon & John Harrold

DANCERS............................Pearl Lang, Andrea Downing, Margaret Cuddy, Polly Welch, Diane Chadwicke, Ruth Miller, Lu Lanterbart, Margaretta DeValera, Lynn Joelson, Sonia Joroff, Elena Salamatova, Marjory Svetlik; Ernest Richman, Tom Avera, Larry Evers, Ralph Linn, Tony Matthews & David Ahdar

CHARACTERS

(in order of appearance)

BILLY BIGELOW

MRS. MULLIN

JUGGLER

DAVID BASCOMBE

CARRIE PIPPERIDGE

JULIE JORDAN

1ST POLICEMAN

NETTIE FOWLER

ENOCH SNOW

JIGGER CRAIGIN

ARMINY

2ND POLICEMAN CAPTAIN

1ST HEAVENLY FRIEND – Brother Joshua

2ND HEAVENLY FRIEND

STARKEEPER

LOUISE

CARNIVAL BOY

ENOCH SNOW, JR.

PRINCIPAL

DR. SELDON

MUSICAL SYNOPSIS

ACT I

"Prologue (The Carousel Waltz)"............................Orchestra

"Mister Snow".. Carrie & Julie

"If I Loved You" ....Billy & Julie

"June is Bustin' Out All Over" .... Nettie, Carrie & Chorus

"Mister Snow – Reprise"....................... Carrie, Enoch & Girls

"When the Children are Asleep" ....Enoch & Carrie

"Blow High, Blow Low" .... Jigger, Billy & Men

"Hornpipe" .... Chorus

"Soliloquy".. Billy

"Finale Act I"...................................Nettie & Company

ACT II

"A Real Nice Clambake" .... Nettie, Julie, Carrie, Enoch & Chorus

"Geraniums in the Winder"................................Enoch

"Stonecutters Cut it on Stone"......................Jigger & Chorus

"What's the Use of Wond'rin'?" .... Julie & Girls

"You'll Never Walk Alone" .... Julie & Nettie

"The Highest Judge of All"................................... Billy

"Ballet"........ Louise, Carnival Boy, Enoch, Snow Children & Dancers

"Carrie's Incidental"..Carrie

"Porch Scene (If I Loved You – Reprise)" .... Billy

"Finale Ultimo (You'll Never Walk Alone – Reprise)".........Company

AGNES DE MILLE:
THE DANCES OF *CAROUSEL*

In the last year of her life, legendary choreographer Agnes de Mille revisited her contributions to the original groundbreaking 1945 Broadway production of *Rodgers & Hammerstein's CAROUSEL*, resulting in an extraordinary video of insight, commentary and recollection. Hosted by the composer's daughter, Mary Rodgers, the video includes the dance sequences from "June is Bustin' Out All Over," "The Hornpipe," and the Act II Ballet, recreated by Ms. de Mille's longtime associate Gemze de Lappe and performed by members of the Nashville Ballet. Commentary from Ms. de Mille and Ms. de Lappe includes analysis, discussion and demonstration; advice and suggestions for the director; and discussion of sets, costumes and lighting. This instructional video is included with the licensing materials provided for *CAROUSEL* and is recommended for viewing by your entire production team, cast and crew.

ACT I

(The time is late afternoon. Extending from stage right to the center is a merry-go-round labeled "Mullin's Carousel." Below the merry-go-round, right center, is the stand of **BILLY BIGELOW**, *the barker for the carousel. Left center is the ticket-seller's stand where* **MRS. MULLIN** *herself presides. Up on the extreme left is a platform backed by an ornate show tent occupied by "The Beauties of Europe." Below this platform, down left, is another stand occupied by the barker for the "Beauties." The two barker stands are elevated so that these two characters can be easily seen above the heads of the crowd.* **MRS. MULLIN** *is seated on a high stool behind her stand so that she is also visible at all times. Downstage extreme right is a Hoky Poky Ice Cream wagon; a* **MAN** *standing upstage from it is selling ice-cream cornucopias.)*

(NOTE: This scene is set to the music of a waltz suite. The only sound comes from the orchestra pit. The pantomimic action is synchronized to the music, but it is in no sense a ballet treatment.)

1

[MUSIC NO. 01 "PROLOGUE (THE CAROUSEL WALTZ)"]

(At measure 27 of the music the lights bleed through the scrim to reveal a tableau. At measure 50 the scrim rises and on the downbeat of measure 51 the entire scene comes to life. At rise: FISHERMEN, SAILORS, their WIVES, CHILDREN, GIRLS from the local mill, and other types of a coastal town are seen moving about the park, patronizing the various concessions and in general "seeing the sights." The carousel is in full motion as the curtain rises, the "Three Beauties of Europe" are dancing on the platform, a JUGGLER is busy juggling downstage left. BILLY is standing downstage of his stand and leaning against it, watching the proceedings. The whole stage seems to be alive and everyone is having a good time.)

(Almost immediately we see the JUGGLER cross to the center of the stage to spin a hat on one stick and a plate on the other. As he does this the carousel comes to a stop. The RIDERS descend from their horses and leave the platform in all directions to mill around with the crowd. The "Three Beauties of Europe" stop dancing. They slip into robes for their rest period. One KID on the carousel during all this movement has stubbornly clung to his horse, and neither his MOTHER nor his BIG SISTER can get him off. The SISTER, a tattle-tale type, skips happily across to her FATHER, who is talking to another gentleman. She pulls at his sleeve and points to her rebellious brother DAVID. MR. BASCOMBE, a formidable fellow with sideburns on his

cheeks and a heavy gold watch-chain across his belly, starts out with his daughter to aid his wife against his recalcitrant son. When he gets there he stands in back of **DAVID, JR.** *with that stern look he reserves for such occasions. That's all there is to it.* **DAVID** *knows the jig is up. He gets off the horse, and the family now walks across the stage with the pomp that befits the richest clan in the locality. They own the Bascombe Cotton Mills, "a little ways up the river." Several* **PEOPLE** *greet them with respectful awe, and they return a gracious but dignified bow to all.)*

(The **JUGGLER***, center stage, has by this time stopped juggling and one of the* **DANCERS** *on the platform has come down and is passing a hat among the crowd for a little collection. As the* **JUGGLER** *goes back to his corner down left, we see a* **GIRL** *and a* **SAILOR** *enter from right. They cross down in front of* **BILLY***, and as they pass him the* **GIRL** *turns to look at* **BILLY***. She decides she wants to talk to him, so she crosses to her* **SAILOR** *friend and asks him to buy her some ice cream. The* **SAILOR** *crosses to the ice cream wagon to buy the cones, and as he does, the* **GIRL** *crosses to* **BILLY** *and talks to him. The* **SAILOR***, having bought the cones, crosses back to the spot where he was, but sees no* **GIRL***. He turns upstage, sees her flirting with* **BILLY***. Crossing up between the two, he looks angrily at* **BILLY***, turns to his* **GIRL***, and tells her to hold the cones. She does. The* **SAILOR** *turns to* **BILLY** *and is just about to take a good sock at him when he notices that* **BILLY** *towers over him.* **BILLY** *smiles and the* **SAILOR***'s look is now one of "I'd better leave this guy alone." He saunters off to the left*

with his **GIRL. BILLY** *then crosses up to* **MRS. MULLIN,** *as a small group of adoring young* **FEMALES** *follows his every movement with worshipful eyes.* **MRS. MULLIN** *is completely mollified by the little attention and gives him a nice big hug.)*

*(***CARRIE** *and* **JULIE** *enter from down left [measure 227].* **CARRIE** *is a naïve, direct, and normal young woman, of the period.* **JULIE** *is more complex, quieter and deeper. They look around at the gay sights, two mill girls on an afternoon off.* **JULIE** *crosses to right center.* **CARRIE** *is mixing in with the crowd left center when* **BILLY** *crosses to go back to his stand down right. On the way he nearly bumps into* **JULIE.** *Their eyes meet for a moment. Then he goes on.)*

(About this time the **BARKER** *of "The Beauties of Europe" comes out and gets on his stand and tries to attract the crowd by pointing to his weary* **DANCERS.** *But now* **BILLY** *starts his spiel [measure 235] and the entire stageful turns toward him and the carousel while* **MRS. MULLIN,** *the proprietress, beams above them. Everyone on the stage starts to sway unconsciously with the rhythm of* **BILLY***'s words (unheard by the audience) [measure 251] – all but* **JULIE. JULIE** *just stands, looking at him over the heads of the others, her gaze steady, her body motionless.* **BILLY** *becomes conscious of her. He looks curiously at her. She takes his mind off his work. He mechanically repeats the spiel. The heads turned up at him now follow his eyes and turn slowly toward* **JULIE.** *This is also the direction of "The Beauties of Europe," and*

the enterprising barker of that attraction immediately takes advantage of this and starts his dancers dancing feverishly, doing bumps that they probably learned at Coney Island. The crowd is now completely "Beauty"-conscious. BILLY is JULIE-conscious and gets down off his stand. MRS. MULLIN, realizing the situation, runs over to BILLY and seems to shout at him.)

(BILLY comes to. His barker's pride reawakened, he mounts his stand and proceeds to win back his public. He starts his regular spiel. The GIRLS all turn back to BILLY and sway with his rhythm again. Some of the MEN go along with the "Beauties" – all except the ones whose WIVES pull them away.)

(When BILLY finishes, there is a stampede of GIRLS to buy tickets for the carousel. JULIE tries too, but she gets crowded out. BILLY notices this; pretty soon there will be no more places left. He smiles and with exaggerated gallantry walks over to her and offers his arm. With a frightened little grin she accepts it and he leads her grandly toward the carousel. MRS. MULLIN, her nose out of joint, yells at JULIE, motioning to her that she wants her five-cent fare.)

(JULIE fumbles in her purse. After some delay, occasioned by her excitement, she finally produces a nickel. Then MRS. MULLIN takes her time about giving her a ticket. In fact, she stalls until the carousel actually gets started. When she has her ticket, JULIE dashes back to the carousel. It is going slowly and she is afraid to get on. BILLY laughs and

suddenly lifts her up and puts her on the only
remaining horse on the carousel.)

(It must be understood that **BILLY***'s attitude*
to **JULIE** *throughout the scene is one of only*
casual and laconic interest. He can get all the
girls he wants. One is like another. This one
is a cute little thing. Like hundreds of others.)

(Once he has got her on the carousel, he
dismisses her from his mind. He turns back
to **MRS. MULLIN,** *but for some reason that*
lady gives him an icy glare. He shrugs his
shoulders, looks again to the carousel, and
collects the tickets from the people seated on
the various animals. **JULIE** *comes around*
again. He waves at her patronizingly. It
means nothing to him. She waves back. It
means so much to her that she nearly falls off!
He laughs. The carousel is revolving faster
now, but he hops on and leans against the
horse on which **JULIE** *is seated.* **MRS. MULLIN,**
seeing this, is so furious that she gets down
from her stand and starts to pace the stage
angrily. Great excitement is stirring down
right. A group of **KIDS** *herald the approach of*
a bear being led onstage by a ballerina in a
short ruffly skirt. [The bear is a **SMALL MAN**
in a well-made bearskin.].)

(Arriving stage center, the **GIRL** *in the ruffly*
skirt executes a few dance steps. Then, to the
great delight of all, the bear does exactly the
same steps. A **CLOWN** *now enters from down*
right, goes onstage next to the bear, and does
some acrobatic tricks. The **JUGGLER** *starts*
juggling again, the **DANCERS** *dance. The*
entire stage is in a bedlam of excitement, the

carousel keeps turning at full speed, **BILLY** *is leaning closer to* **JULIE**, *the music rises in an ecstatic crescendo, but the lights, as if they sensed that we have accomplished all we wanted to in this scene, black out and the curtains close.)*

[MUSIC NO. 02 "CHANGE OF SCENE"]

Scene Two:
A Tree-Lined Path Along The Shore,
A Few Minutes Later

[MUSIC NO. 03 "OPENING ACT I, SCENE TWO"]

(Near sundown. Through the trees the lights of the amusement park can be seen on the curves of the bay. The music of the merry-go-round is heard faintly in the distance. There is a park bench just right of center. Soon after the curtain opens, CARRIE backs on to the stage from down right.)

CARRIE. C'mon, Julie, it's gettin' late... Julie!

(JULIE enters right.)

That's right! Don't you pay her no mind.

(Looking offstage.)

Look! She's comin' around at you again. Let's run!

JULIE. *(Holding her ground.)* I ain't skeered o' her.

(But she is a little.)

MRS. MULLIN. *(Entering, in no mood to be trifled with.)* I got one more thing to tell you, young woman. If y'ever so much as poke your nose in my carousel again, you'll be thrown out. Right on your little pink behind!

CARRIE. You got no call t'talk t'her like that! She ain't doin' you no harm.

MRS. MULLIN. Oh, ain't she? Think I wanta get in trouble with the police and lose my license?

JULIE. *(To CARRIE.)* What *is* the woman talkin' about?

MRS. MULLIN. *(Scornfully.)* Lettin' my barker fool with you! Ain't you ashamed?

JULIE. I don't let no man...

MRS. MULLIN. *(To* CARRIE.*)* He leaned against her all through the ride.

JULIE. *(To* CARRIE.*)* He leaned against the horse. *(To* MRS. MULLIN.*)* But he didn't lay a hand on me!

MRS. MULLIN. Oh no, Miss Innercence! And he didn't put his arm around yer waist neither.

CARRIE. And suppose he did. Is that reason to hev a capuluptic fit?

MRS. MULLIN. You keep out o' this, you rip! *(To* JULIE.*)* You've had my warnin'. If you come back you'll be thrown out!

JULIE. Who'll throw me out?

MRS. MULLIN. Billy Bigelow – the barker. Same feller you let get so free with you.

JULIE. I... I bet he wouldn't. He wouldn't throw me out!

CARRIE. I bet the same thing.

> *(***BILLY BIGELOW*** enters, followed by two* GIRLS. *He hears and sees the argument; he turns and tells the* GIRLS *to leave. They exit.)*

MRS. MULLIN. *(To* CARRIE.*)* You mind yer business, hussy!

CARRIE. Go back to yer carousel and leave us alone!

JULIE. Yes. Leave us alone, y'old...y'old...

MRS. MULLIN. I don't run my business for a lot o' chippies.

CARRIE. Chippie, yerself!

JULIE. Yes, chippie yerself!

BILLY. *(Shouting.) Shut up!* Jabber, jabber, jabber...!

> *(They stand before him like three guilty schoolgirls. He makes his voice shrill to imitate them.)*

Jabber, jabber, jabber, jabber, jabber... What's goin' on anyway? Spittin' and sputt'rin' – like three lumps of corn poppin' on a shovel!

JULIE. Mr. Bigelow, please –

BILLY. Don't yell!

JULIE. *(Backing away a step.)* I didn't yell.

BILLY. Well...don't. *(To* MRS. MULLIN.*)* What's the matter?

MRS. MULLIN. Take a look at that girl, Billy. She ain't ever to be allowed on my carousel again. Next time she tries to get in – if she ever dares – I want you to throw her out! Understand? Throw her out!

BILLY. *(Turning to* JULIE.*)* All right. You heard what the lady said. Run home now.

CARRIE. C'mon, Julie.

JULIE. *(Looking at* BILLY, *amazed.)* No, I won't.

MRS. MULLIN. *(To* BILLY.*)* Like a drink?

BILLY. Sure.

JULIE. *(Speaking very earnestly, as if it meant a great deal to her.)* Mr. Bigelow, tell me please – honest and truly – if I came to the carousel, would you throw me out?

> *(He looks at* MRS. MULLIN, *then at* JULIE, *then back at* MRS. MULLIN.*)*

BILLY. What did she do, anyway?

JULIE. She says you put your arm around my waist.

BILLY. *(The light dawning on him.)* So that's it!

> *(Turning to* MRS. MULLIN.*)*

Here's something new! Can't put my arm around a girl without I ask your permission! That how it is?

MRS. MULLIN. *(For the first time on the defensive.)* I just don't want *that* one around no more.

BILLY. *(Turning to* **JULIE.***)* You come around all you want, see? And if y'ain't got the price, Billy Bigelow'll treat you to a ride.

MRS. MULLIN. Big talker, ain't you, Mr. Bigelow? I suppose you think I can't throw *you* out too, if I wanta!

> *(***BILLY***, ignoring her, looks straight ahead of him, complacently.)*

You're such a good barker I can't get along without you. That it? Well, just for that you're discharged. Your services are no longer required. You're bounced! See?

BILLY. Very well, Mrs. Mullin.

MRS. MULLIN. *(In retreat.)* You know I *could* bounce you if I felt like it!

BILLY. And you felt like it just now. So I'm bounced.

MRS. MULLIN. Do you have to pick up every word I say? I only said...

BILLY. That my services were no longer required. Very good. We'll let it go at that, Mrs. Mullin.

MRS. MULLIN. All right, you devil! *(Shouting.)* We'll let it go at that!

JULIE. Mr. Bigelow, if she's willin' to say she'll change her mind...

BILLY. You keep out of it.

JULIE. I don't want this to happen 'count of me.

BILLY. *(Suddenly, to* **MRS. MULLIN***, pointing at* **JULIE***.)* Apologize to her!

CARRIE. A-ha!

MRS. MULLIN. Me apologize to *her*! Fer what? Fer spoilin' the good name of my carousel – the business that was left to me by my dear, saintly, departed husband, Mr. Mullin?

(Led toward tears by her own eloquence.)

I only wish my poor husband was alive this minute.

BILLY. I bet *he* don't.

MRS. MULLIN. He'd give you such a smack on the jaw...!

BILLY. That's just what *I'm* goin' to give you if you don't dry up!

(He advances threateningly.)

MRS. MULLIN. *(Backing away.)* You upstart! After all I done for you! Now I'm through with you for good! Y'hear?

BILLY. *(Making as if to take a swipe at her with the back of his hand.) Get!*

MRS. MULLIN. *(As she goes off.)* Through fer good! I won't take you back like before!

> *(**BILLY** watches her go, then crosses back to **JULIE**. There is a moment of awkward silence.)*

CARRIE. Mr. Bigelow –

BILLY. Don't get sorry for me or I'll give *you* a slap on the jaw!

> *(More silence. He looks at **JULIE**. She lowers her eyes.)*

And don't *you* feel sorry for me either!

JULIE. *(Frightened.)* I don't feel sorry for you, Mr. Bigelow.

BILLY. You're a liar, you *are* feelin' sorry for me. I can see it in your face.

> *(Faces front, throws out chest, proud.)*

You think, now that she fired me, I won't be able to get another job...

JULIE. What *will* you do now, Mr. Bigelow?

BILLY. First of all, I'll go get myself...a glass of beer. Whenever anything bothers me I always drink a glass of beer.

JULIE. Then you *are* bothered about losing your job!

BILLY. No. Only about how I'm goin' t'pay fer the beer. *(To* **CARRIE**, *gesturing with right hand.)* Will *you* pay for it?

*(***CARRIE*** looks doubtful. He speaks to* **JULIE***.)*

Will you?

*(***JULIE*** doesn't answer.)*

How much money have you got?

JULIE. Forty-three cents.

BILLY. *(To* **CARRIE***.)* And you?

*(***CARRIE*** lowers her eyes and turns left.)*

I asked you how much you've got?

*(***CARRIE*** begins to weep softly.)*

Uh, I understand. Well, you needn't cry about it. I'm goin' to the carousel to get my things. Stay here till I come back. Then we'll go have a drink.

*(***JULIE*** is fumbling for change. She holds it up to* **BILLY***.)*

It's all right.

(He pushes her hand gently away.)

Keep your money, I'll pay.

(He exits whistling down right. **JULIE** *continues to look silently off at the departing figure of* **BILLY**. **CARRIE** *studies her for a*

moment, then crosses to bench left of **JULIE**
and sits.)

[MUSIC NO. 04 "MISTER SNOW"]

CARRIE. *(Spoken in rhythm, timidly.)* JULIE –

(No answer.)

(Spoken in rhythm.) JULIE – DO YOU LIKE HIM?

JULIE. *(Dreaming, spoken in rhythm.)* I DUNNO.

*(***JULIE** *sits on bench.)*

CARRIE. *(Spoken in rhythm.)* DID YOU LIKE IT WHEN HE
TALKED TO YOU TODAY?
WHEN HE PUT YOU ON THE CAROUSEL, THAT WAY?
DID YOU LIKE THAT?

JULIE. *(Spoken in rhythm.)* 'DRUTHER NOT SAY.

CARRIE. *(Shakes her head and chides her, sung.)*
YOU'RE A QUEER ONE, JULIE JORDAN!
YOU ARE QUIETER AND DEEPER THAN A WELL,
AND YOU NEVER TELL ME NOTHIN' –

JULIE.
THERE'S NOTHIN' THAT I KEER T'CHOOSE T'TELL!

CARRIE.
YOU BEEN ACTIN' MOST PECULIAR;
EV'RY MORNIN' YOU'RE AWAKE AHEAD OF ME,
ALW'YS SETTIN' BY THE WINDER –

JULIE.
I LIKE TO WATCH THE RIVER MEET THE SEA.

CARRIE.
WHEN WE WORK IN THE MILL, WEAVIN' AT THE LOOM,
Y'GAZE ABSENT-MINDED AT THE ROOF,
AND HALF THE TIME YER SHUTTLE GETS TWISTED IN THE
    THREADS
TILL Y'CAN'T TELL THE WARP FROM THE WOOF!

JULIE. *(Looking away and smiling. She knows it's true.)*
'TAIN'T SO!

CARRIE.
YOU'RE A QUEER ONE, JULIE JORDAN!
YOU WON'T EVER TELL A BODY WHAT YOU THINK.
YOU'RE AS TIGHT-LIPPED AS AN OYSTER,
AND AS SILENT AS AN OLD SAHAIRA SPINK!

(The music continues under dialogue.)

JULIE. *(Spoken in rhythm.)* SPINX.

CARRIE. Huh?

JULIE. Spinx.

CARRIE. Uh-uh. Spink.

JULIE. Y'spell it with an "x."

CARRIE. That's only when there's more than one.

JULIE. *(Out-bluffed.)* Oh.

CARRIE. *(Looking sly.)* Julie, I been bustin' t'tell *you* somethin' lately.

JULIE. Y'hev?

CARRIE. Reason I didn't keer t'tell you before was 'cause you didn't hev a feller of yer own. Now y'got one, I ken tell y'about mine.

JULIE. *(Quietly and thoughtfully.)* I'm glad you got a feller, Carrie. What's his name?

CARRIE. *(Now she sings, almost reverently.)*
HIS NAME IS MISTER SNOW,
AND AN UPSTANDIN' MAN IS HE.
HE COMES HOME EV'RY NIGHT IN HIS ROUND-BOTTOMED BOAT
WITH A NET FULL OF HERRING FROM THE SEA.
AN ALMOST PERFECT BEAU,
AS REFINED AS A GIRL COULD WISH,

BUT HE SPENDS SO MUCH TIME IN HIS ROUND-
    BOTTOMED BOAT,
THAT HE CAN'T SEEM TO LOSE THE SMELL OF FISH.
THE FUST TIME HE KISSED ME, THE WHIFF OF HIS CLO'ES
KNOCKED ME FLAT ON THE FLOOR OF THE ROOM;
BUT NOW THAT I LOVE HIM, MY HEART'S IN MY NOSE,
AND FISH IS MY FAV'RITE PERFUME.
LAST NIGHT HE SPOKE QUITE LOW,
AND A FAIR-SPOKEN MAN IS HE,

(Memorizing exactly what he said.)

AND HE SAID, "MISS PIPPERIDGE, I'D LIKE IT FINE
IF I COULD BE WED WITH A WIFE.
AND, INDEED, MISS PIPPERIDGE, IF YOU'LL BE MINE,
I'LL BE YOURS FER THE REST OF MY LIFE!"
NEXT MOMENT WE WERE PROMISED
AND NOW MY MIND'S IN A MAZE,
FER ALL I KEN DO IS LOOK FORWARD TO
THAT WONDERFUL DAY OF DAYS...
WHEN I MARRY MISTER SNOW,
THE FLOWERS'LL BE BUZZIN' WITH THE HUM OF BEES,
THE BIRDS'LL MAKE A RACKET IN THE CHURCHYARD
    TREES,
WHEN I MARRY MISTER SNOW.
THEN IT'S OFF TO HOME WE'LL GO,
AND BOTH OF US'LL LOOK A LITTLE DREAMY-EYED,
A-DRIVIN' TO A COTTAGE BY THE OCEANSIDE
WHERE THE SALTY BREEZES BLOW.
HE'LL CARRY ME 'CROSS THE THRESHOLD,
AND I'LL BE AS MEEK AS A LAMB.
THEN HE'LL SET ME ON MY FEET,
AND I'LL SAY, KINDA SWEET:
(Spoken in rhythm.) "WELL, MISTER SNOW, HERE I AM!"
(Sung.) THEN I'LL KISS HIM SO HE'LL KNOW
THAT EV'RYTHIN'LL BE AS RIGHT AS RIGHT KEN BE,

A-LIVIN' IN A COTTAGE BY THE SEA WITH ME,
FOR I LOVE THAT MISTER SNOW –
THAT YOUNG, SEAFARIN', BOLD AND DARIN',
BIG, BEWHISKERED, OVERBEARIN'
DARLIN', MISTER SNOW!

>*(She looks soulfully ahead of her, and sits down, in a trance of her own making.)*

JULIE. Carrie! I'm so happy fer you!

CARRIE. So y'see I ken understand now how *you* feel about Billy Bigelow.

>*(**BILLY** enters down right, carrying a suitcase and with a coat on his arm. He puts the suitcase down and the coat on top of it.)*

BILLY. You still here?

>*(They both rise, looking at **BILLY**.)*

CARRIE. You *told* us to wait fer you.

BILLY. What you think I want with two of you? I meant that *one* of you was to wait. The other can go home.

CARRIE. All right.

JULIE. *(Almost simultaneously.)* All right.

>*(They look at each other, then at **BILLY**, smiling inanely.)*

BILLY. One of you goes home. *(To **CARRIE**.)* Where do you work?

CARRIE. Bascombe's Cotton Mill, a little ways up the river.

BILLY. And you?

JULIE. I work there, too.

BILLY. Well, one of you goes home. Which of you *wants* to stay?

(No answer.)

Come on, speak up! Which of you stays?

CARRIE. Whoever stays loses her job.

BILLY. How do you mean?

CARRIE. All Bascombe's girls hev to be respectable. We all hev to live in the mill boardinghouse, and if we're late they lock us out and we can't go back to work there any more.

BILLY. Is that true? Will they bounce you if you're not home on time?

*(Both **GIRLS** nod.)*

JULIE. That's right.

CARRIE. Julie, should I go?

JULIE. I...can't tell you what to do.

CARRIE. All right – you stay, if y'like.

BILLY. That right, you'll be discharged if you stay?

*(**JULIE** nods.)*

CARRIE. Julie, should I go?

JULIE. *(Embarrassed.)* Why do you keep askin' me that?

CARRIE. You know what's best to do.

JULIE. *(Profoundly moved, slowly.)* All right, Carrie, you can go home.

> *(Pause. Then reluctantly **CARRIE** starts off. As she gets left center, she turns and says, uncertainly:)*

CARRIE. Well, good night.

> *(She waits a moment to see if **JULIE** will follow her. **JULIE** doesn't move. **CARRIE** exits.)*

BILLY. *(Speaking as he crosses to left center.)* Now we're both out of a job.

(No answer. He whistles softly.)

Have you had your supper?

JULIE. No.

BILLY. Want to eat out on the pier?

JULIE. No.

BILLY. Anywheres else?

JULIE. No.

(He whistles a few more bars. He sits on the bench, looking her over, up and down.)

BILLY. You don't come to the carousel much. Only see you three times before today.

JULIE. *(Breathless, she crosses to bench and sits beside him.)* I been there much more than that.

BILLY. That right? Did you see me?

JULIE. Yes.

BILLY. Did you know I was Billy Bigelow?

JULIE. They told me.

(He whistles again, then turns to her.)

BILLY. Have you got a sweetheart?

JULIE. No.

BILLY. Ah, don't lie to me.

JULIE. I heven't anybody.

BILLY. You stayed here with me the first time I asked you. You know your way around all right, all right!

JULIE. No, I don't Mr. Bigelow.

BILLY. And I suppose you don't know why you're sittin' here – like this – alone with me. You wouldn' of stayed so quick if you hadna done it before... What did you stay for anyway?

JULIE. So you wouldn't be left alone.

BILLY. Alone! God, you're dumb! I don't need to be alone. I can have all the girls I want. Don't you know that?

JULIE. I know, Mr. Bigelow.

BILLY. What do you know?

JULIE. That all the girls are crazy fer you. But that's not why *I* stayed. I stayed because you been so good to me.

BILLY. Well, then you can go home.

JULIE. I don't want to go home now.

BILLY. And suppose I go away and leave you sittin' here?

JULIE. Even then I wouldn't go home.

BILLY. Do you know what you remind me of? A girl I knew in Coney Island. Tell you how I met her. One night at closin' time – we had put out the lights in the carousel, and just as I was –

> *(He breaks off suddenly as, during the above speech, a* **POLICEMAN** *has entered from down left and comes across stage.* **BILLY** *instinctively takes on an attitude of guilty silence. The* **POLICEMAN** *frowns down at them as he walks by.* **BILLY** *follows him with his eyes.)*

> *(At the same time that the* **POLICEMAN** *entered from left,* **MR. BASCOMBE** *has come in from right. He flourishes his cane and breathes in the night air as if he enjoyed it.)*

POLICEMAN. Evenin', Mr. Bascombe.

BASCOMBE. Good evening, Timony. Nice night.

POLICEMAN. 'Deed it is. *(Conspiritorially.)* Er... Mr. Bascombe. That one of your girls?

BASCOMBE. *(Taken aback, in a low voice.)* One of *my* girls?

> *(The **POLICEMAN** nods. **BASCOMBE** crosses in front of the **POLICEMAN** to the right of **JULIE** and peers at her in the darkness.)*

Is that *you*, Miss Jordan?

JULIE. Yes, Mr. Bascombe.

BASCOMBE. What ever are you doing out at this hour?

JULIE. I... I...

BASCOMBE. You know what time we close our doors at the mill boardinghouse. You couldn't be home on time now if you ran all the way.

JULIE. No, sir.

BILLY. *(To **JULIE**.)* Who's old sideburns?

POLICEMAN. Here, now! Don't you go t'callin' Mr. Bascombe names – 'less you're fixin' t'git yerself into trouble.

> *(**BILLY** shuts up. Policemen have this effect on him. The **POLICEMAN** turns to **BASCOMBE**.)*

We got a report on this feller from the police chief at Bangor. He's a pretty sly gazaybo. Come up from Coney Island.

BASCOMBE. *(Knowingly.)* New York, eh?

POLICEMAN. He works on carousels, makes a specialty of young things like this'n. Gets 'em all moony-eyed. Promises to marry 'em, then takes their money.

JULIE. *(Promptly and brightly.)* I ain't got no money.

POLICEMAN. Speak when you're spoken to, miss!

BASCOMBE. Julie, you've heard what kind of blackguard this man is. You're an inexperienced girl and he's imposed on you and deluded you. That's why I'm inclined to give you one more chance.

POLICEMAN. *(To* **JULIE.***)* Y'hear that?

BASCOMBE. I'm meeting Mrs. Bascombe at the church. We'll drive you home and I'll explain everything to the house matron.

> *(He holds out his hand.)*

Come, my child.

> *(But she doesn't move.)*

POLICEMAN. Well, girl! Don't be settin' there like you didn't hev good sense!

JULIE. Do I *hev* to go with you?

BASCOMBE. No. You don't have to.

JULIE. Then I'll stay.

POLICEMAN. After I warned you!

BASCOMBE. You see, Timony! There are some of them you just can't help. Good night!

> *(He exits.)*

POLICEMAN. Good night, Mr. Bascombe.

> *(He looks down at* **BILLY**, *starts to go, then turns to* **BILLY** *and speaks.)*

You! You low-down scalawag! I oughta throw you in jail.

BILLY. What for?

> *(After a pause.)*

POLICEMAN. Dunno. Wish I did.

> (*He exits.* **BILLY** *looks after him.*)

JULIE. Well, and *then* what?

BILLY. Huh?

JULIE. You were startin' to tell me a story.

BILLY. Me?

JULIE. About that girl in Coney Island. You said you just put out the lights in the carousel – that's as far as you got.

BILLY. Oh, yes. Yes, well, just as the lights went out, someone came along. A little girl with a shawl – you know, she... (*Puzzled.*) Say, tell me somethin' – ain't you scared of me?

[MUSIC NO. 05 "IF I LOVED YOU"]

I mean, after what the cop said about me takin' money from girls.

JULIE. I ain't skeered.

BILLY. That your name? Julie? Julie somethin'?

JULIE.
JULIE JORDAN.

> (**BILLY** *whistles reflectively.*)

BILLY. (*Singing softly, shaking his head.*)
YOU'RE A QUEER ONE, JULIE JORDAN.
AIN'T YOU SORRY THAT YOU DIDN'T RUN AWAY?
YOU CAN STILL GO, IF YOU WANTA –

JULIE. (*Singing, looking away so as not to meet his eye.*)
I RECKON THAT I KEER T'CHOOSE T'STAY.
YOU COULDN'T TAKE MY MONEY
IF I DIDN'T HEV ANY,

> AND I DON'T HEV A PENNY, THAT'S TRUE!
> AND IF I DID HEV MONEY
> YOU COULDN'T TAKE ANY
> 'CAUSE YOU'D ASK, AND I'D GIVE IT TO YOU!

BILLY.
> YOU'RE A QUEER ONE, JULIE JORDAN.
> AIN'T Y'EVER HAD A FELLER YOU GIVE MONEY TO?

JULIE. *(Spoken in rhythm.)* NO.

BILLY.
> AIN'T Y'EVER HAD A FELLER AT ALL?

JULIE. *(Spoken in rhythm.)* NO.

BILLY.
> WELL Y'MUSTA HAD A FELLER YOU WENT WALKIN' WITH –

JULIE. *(Spoken in rhythm.)* YES.

BILLY.
> WHERE'D YOU WALK?

JULIE.
> NOWHERE SPECIAL I RECALL.

BILLY.
> IN THE WOODS?

JULIE. *(Spoken in rhythm.)* NO.

BILLY.
> ON THE BEACH?

JULIE. *(Spoken in rhythm.)* NO.

BILLY.
> DID YOU LOVE HIM?

JULIE. *(Spoken in rhythm.)* NO!

> Never loved no one – I *told* you that!

BILLY. Say, you're a funny kid. Want to go into town and dance maybe? Or...

JULIE. No. I hev to be keerful.

BILLY. Of what?

JULIE. My character. Y'see, I'm never goin' to marry.

> I'M NEVER GOIN' TO MARRY.
> IF I WAS GOIN' TO MARRY,
> I WOULDN'T HEV T'BE SECH A STICKLER.
> BUT I'M NEVER GOIN' TO MARRY,
> AND A GIRL WHO DON'T MARRY
> HAS GOT TO BE MUCH MORE PERTICKLER!

BILLY. Suppose I was to say to you that I'd marry you?

JULIE. You?

BILLY. That scares you, don't it? You're thinkin' what that cop said.

JULIE. No, I ain't. I never paid no mind to what he said.

BILLY. But you wouldn't marry anyone like me, would you?

JULIE. Yes, I would, if I loved you. It wouldn't make any difference what you – even if I died fer it.

BILLY. How do you know what you'd do if you loved me? Or how you'd feel – or anythin'?

JULIE. I dunno how I know.

BILLY. Ah –

JULIE. Jest the same, I know how I – how it'd be – if I loved you.

> WHEN I WORKED IN THE MILL, WEAVIN' AT THE LOOM,
> I'D GAZE ABSENT-MINDED AT THE ROOF,
> AND HALF THE TIME THE SHUTTLE'D TANGLE IN THE
>   THREADS,
> AND THE WARP'D GET MIXED WITH THE WOOF...
> IF I LOVED YOU –

BILLY. But you don't.

JULIE. No, I don't. *(Smiles.)*

BUT SOMEHOW I KEN SEE
JEST EXACK'LY HOW I'D BE...
IF I LOVED YOU,
TIME AND AGAIN I WOULD TRY TO SAY
ALL I'D WANT YOU TO KNOW.
IF I LOVED YOU,
WORDS WOULDN'T COME IN AN EASY WAY –
ROUND IN CIRCLES I'D GO!
LONGIN' TO TELL YOU, BUT AFRAID AND SHY,
I'D LET MY GOLDEN CHANCES PASS ME BY!
SOON YOU'D LEAVE ME,
OFF YOU WOULD GO IN THE MIST OF DAY,
NEVER, NEVER TO KNOW
HOW I LOVED YOU –
IF I LOVED YOU.

> *(They sit in silence; he studies her for a moment, then turns away.)*

BILLY. Well, anyway – you don't love me. That's what you said.

JULIE. Yes...

> *(Some blossoms drift down to their feet.)*

I can smell them, can you? The blossoms?

> *(**BILLY** picks some blossoms up and drops them.)*

The wind brings them down.

BILLY. Ain't much wind tonight. Hardly any.

YOU CAN'T HEAR A SOUND – NOT THE TURN OF A LEAF,
NOR THE FALL OF A WAVE HITTIN' THE SAND.
THE TIDE'S CREEPIN' UP ON THE BEACH LIKE A THIEF,

AFRAID TO BE CAUGHT STEALIN' THE LAND.

ON A NIGHT LIKE THIS I START TO WONDER WHAT LIFE IS
ALL ABOUT.

JULIE.

AND I ALWAYS SAY TWO HEADS ARE BETTER THAN ONE,
TO FIGGER IT OUT.

BILLY. I don't need you or anyone to help me. I got it
figgered out for myself. We ain't important. What are
we? A couple of specks of nothin'. Look up there.

(He points up. They both look up.)

THERE'S A HELLUVA LOT O' STARS IN THE SKY,
AND THE SKY'S SO BIG THE SEA LOOKS SMALL,
AND TWO LITTLE PEOPLE –
YOU AND I –
WE DON'T COUNT AT ALL.

*(They are silent for a while, the music
continuing. BILLY looks down at her and
speaks.)*

You're a funny kid. Don't remember ever meetin' a girl
like you.

*(A thought strikes him suddenly. He looks
suspicious, and backs away.)*

You – are you tryin' t'get me to marry you?

JULIE. No!

BILLY. Then what's puttin' it into my head?

*(He thinks it out. She smiles. He looks down
at her.)*

You're different all right. Don't know what it is. You
look up at me with that little kid face like... Like you
trusted me.

(She looks at him steadily, smiling sadly, as if she were sorry for him and wanted to help him. He looks thoughtful, then talks to himself, but audibly.)

I wonder what it'd be like.

JULIE. What?

BILLY. Nothin'. *(To himself again.)* I know what it'd be like. It'd be awful. I can just see myself –

KINDA SCRAWNY AND PALE, PICKIN' AT MY FOOD,
AND LOVESICK LIKE ANY OTHER GUY –
I'D THROW AWAY MY SWEATER AND DRESS UP LIKE A DUDE
IN A DICKEY AND A COLLAR AND A TIE...
IF I LOVED YOU.

JULIE. But you don't.

BILLY. No, I don't. *(Smiles.)*

BUT SOMEHOW I CAN SEE
JUST EXACTLY HOW I'D BE.
IF I LOVED YOU,
TIME AND AGAIN I WOULD TRY TO SAY
ALL I'D WANT YOU TO KNOW.
IF I LOVED YOU,
WORDS WOULDN'T COME IN AN EASY WAY –
ROUND IN CIRCLES I'D GO!
LONGING TO TELL YOU, BUT AFRAID AND SHY,
I'D LET MY GOLDEN CHANCES PASS ME BY.
SOON YOU'D LEAVE ME,
OFF YOU WOULD GO IN THE MIST OF DAY,
NEVER, NEVER TO KNOW
HOW I LOVED YOU –
IF I LOVED YOU.

*(The music continues as he thinks it over
for a few silent moments. Then he shakes his
head ruefully. He turns to JULIE and frowns
at her.)*

I'm not a feller to marry anybody. Even if a girl was
foolish enough to want me to, I wouldn't.

JULIE. *(Looking right up at him.)* Don't worry about it –
Billy.

BILLY. Who's worried!

(She smiles and looks up at the trees.)

JULIE. You're right about there bein' no wind. The blossoms
are jest comin' down by theirselves. Jest their time to,
I reckon.

*(BILLY looks straight ahead of him, a troubled
expression in his eyes. JULIE looks up at him,
smiling, patient. The music rises ecstatically.
He crosses nearer to her and looks down at
her. She doesn't move her eyes from his. He
takes her face in his hands, leans down, and
kisses her gently. The curtains close as the
lights dim.)*

**[MUSIC NO. 06 "OPENING ACT I, SCENE
THREE"]**

Scene Three:
Nettie Fowler's Spa on the Oceanfront in June

(Up right is NETTIE's residence and establishment of gray, weathered clapboard and shingled roof. Just left of the door, on the porch, there is a good-sized arbor, overhung with wisteria. Under the arbor are a table and three chairs. From the house to offstage left platforms are built up and appear to be docks. The backdrop, painted blue, depicts the bay. On the drop is painted a moored ketch and other sailing craft. MEN are carrying bushel baskets of clams and piling them on the dock, preparatory to loading the boats. During the scene more MEN come on. A group stands outside the spa to heckle NETTIE and the WOMEN who are inside, cooking. Other MEN enter and join the hecklers. The music begins to fade as the dialogue continues.)

1ST MAN. Nettie!

2ND MAN. *(Cupping his hands and calling.)* Oh, Nettie Fowler!

NETTIE. *(In the house.)* Hold yer horses!

1ST MAN. Got any of them doughnuts fried yet?

3RD MAN. How 'bout some apple turnovers.

NETTIE. *(Still inside, getting irritated.)* Hold yer horses!

(The MEN laugh, now that they're getting a rise out of her.)

2ND MAN. *(Crossing up to porch.)* Hey, what're you and them women doin' in there?

WOMEN. *(Offstage.)* Hold yer horses!

(The **MEN** *slap their thighs, and one another's backs. This is rich!)*

1ST MAN. Are y'cookin' the ice cream?

(This convulses them. Throws his arm on **3RD MAN**'s *shoulders.)*

3RD MAN. Roastin' the lemonade?

ALL MEN. Nettie Fowler...! Yoo-hoo...! Nettie Fow-w-w-w-ler...!

(Some **WOMEN** *come out of the house.* **CARRIE** *follows, pushing her way through the crowd and coming up front. The* **GIRLS** *carry rolling-pins and spoons – a formidable crowd of angry females interrupted at their work in the kitchen. Their stern looks soon reduce the male laughter to faint snickers and sheepish grins.)*

SEVERAL GIRLS. Will you stop that racket!

CARRIE. Git away you passel o' demons!

1ST MAN. Where's Nettie?

CARRIE. In the kitchen busier'n a bee in a bucket o' tar – and y'oughter be ashamed, makin' yersel's a plague and a nuisance with yer yellin' and screamin' and carryin' on.

[MUSIC NO. 07 "JUNE IS BUSTIN' OUT ALL OVER"]

WOMEN. *(Spoken in rhythm.)* GIVE IT TO 'EM GOOD, CARRIE, GIVE IT TO 'EM GOOD!

CARRIE.
GET AWAY, YOU NO-ACCOUNT NOTHIN'S
WITH YER SILLY JOKES AND PRATTLE!

IF Y'PACKED ALL YER BRAINS IN A BUTTERFLY'S HEAD
THEY'D STILL HEV ROOM TO RATTLE.

WOMEN. *(Spoken in rhythm.)* GIVE IT TO 'EM GOOD, CARRIE,
GIVE IT TO 'EM GOOD!
TELL 'EM SOMETHIN' THAT'LL L'ARN 'EM!

CARRIE.

GET AWAY, YOU ROUSTABOUT RIFF-RAFF
WITH YER BELLIES FULL OF GROG.
IF Y'PACKED ALL YER BRAINS IN A POLLYWOG'S HEAD,
HE'D NEVER EVEN GROW TO BE A FROG!

WOMEN.

THE POLLYWOG'D NEVER BE A FROG!
(Spoken in rhythm.) THAT'LL L'ARN 'EM,
DARN 'EM!

MEN.

NOW JEST A MINUTE, LADIES,
YOU GOT NO CALL TO FRET.
WE ONLY ASKED PERLITELY
IF YOU WAS READY YET.
WE'D KINDA LIKE THIS CLAMBAKE
TO GET AN EARLY START,
AND WANTED FER TO TELL YOU
WE WENT AND DONE OUR PART.

BASSES. *(Pointing to pile of baskets.)*
LOOK AT THEM CLAMS!

BARITONES.

BEEN DIGGIN' 'EM SINCE SUNUP!

BASSES.

LOOK AT THEM CLAMS!

2ND TENORS.

ALL READY FER THE BOATS.

BASSES.

LOOK AT THEM CLAMS!

1ST TENORS.

WE'RE ALL WORE OUT AND DONE UP –

ALL MEN.

AND WHAT'S MORE, WE'RE HUNGRY AS GOATS!

ALL WOMEN.

YOU'LL GET NO DRINKS ER VITTLES
TILL WE GET ACROSS THE BAY,
SO PULL IN YER BELTS AND LOAD THEM BOATS
AND LET'S GET UNDERWAY.
THE SOONER WE SAIL, THE SOONER WE START
THE CLAMBAKE 'CROSS THE BAY!

> *(The music continues as they snap their fingers and turn. But the* **BOYS'** *attention has been caught by the entrance of* **NETTIE**, *coming out of the house carrying a tray piled high with doughnuts. She is followed by a* **LITTLE GIRL**, *carrying a large tray of coffee cups.)*

NETTIE. Here, boys! Here's some doughnuts and coffee. Fall to!

> *(Crosses to center.)*

MEN. *(As they fall to, speeches overlapping.)* Doughnuts, hooray...! That's our Nettie...! Yer heart's in the right place, Nettie...! Lemme in there...! Quit yer shovin'...!

NETTIE. Here now, don't jump at it like you was a lotta animals in a menag'ry!

> *(She laughs as she crosses over to the* **GIRLS.**)

WOMEN. Nettie...! After us jest tellin' 'em...! Watchere doin' that fer...?

NETTIE. They been diggin' clams since five this mornin' – I see 'em myself, down on the beach.

WOMEN. After the way they been pesterin' and annoyin' you...!

CARRIE. Nettie, yer a soft-hearted ninny!

NETTIE. Oh, y'can't blame 'em. First clambake o' the year
they're always like this. It's like unlockin' a door, and
all the crazy notions they kep' shet up fer the winter
come whoopin' out into the sunshine. This year's jest
like ev'ry other.

> MARCH WENT OUT LIKE A LION,
> A-WHIPPIN' UP THE WATER IN THE BAY.
> THEN APRIL CRIED
> AND STEPPED ASIDE,
> AND ALONG COME PRETTY LITTLE MAY!
> MAY WAS FULL OF PROMISES
> BUT SHE DIDN'T KEEP 'EM QUICK ENOUGH FER SOME,
> AND A CROWD OF DOUBTIN' THOMASES
> WAS PREDICTIN' THAT THE SUMMER'D NEVER COME!

MEN.

> BUT IT'S COMIN', BY GUM!
> Y'KEN FEEL IT COME!
> Y'KEN FEEL IT IN YER HEART,
> Y'KEN SEE IT IN THE GROUND!

WOMEN.

> Y'KEN HEAR IT IN THE TREES,
> Y'KEN SMELL IT IN THE BREEZE –

ALL.

> LOOK AROUND, LOOK AROUND, LOOK AROUND!

NETTIE.

> JUNE IS BUSTIN' OUT ALL OVER,
> ALL OVER THE MEADOW AND THE HILL!
> BUDS'RE BUSTIN' OUTA BUSHES,
> AND THE ROMPIN' RIVER PUSHES
> EV'RY LITTLE WHEEL THAT WHEELS BESIDE A MILL.

ALL.

> JUNE IS BUSTIN' OUT ALL OVER.

NETTIE.

 THE FEELIN' IS GETTIN' SO INTENSE
 THAT THE YOUNG VIRGINIA CREEPERS
 HEV BEEN HUGGIN' THE BEJEEPERS
 OUTA ALL THE MORNIN'-GLORIES ON THE FENCE!
 BECAUSE IT'S JUNE!

WOMEN & MEN.

 JUNE – JUNE – JUNE –

ALL.

 JEST BECAUSE IT'S JUNE – JUNE – JUNE!

NETTIE.

 FRESH AND ALIVE AND GAY AND YOUNG,
 JUNE IS A LOVE SONG, SWEETLY SUNG.

ALL. *(Softly.)*

 JUNE IS BUSTIN' OUT ALL OVER!

1ST MAN.

 THE SAPLIN'S ARE BUSTIN' OUT WITH SAP!

1ST WOMAN.

 LOVE HAS FOUND MY BROTHER, JUNIOR.

2ND MAN.

 AND MY SISTER'S EVEN LUNIER!

2ND WOMAN.

 AND MY MA IS GETTIN' KITTENISH WITH PAP!

ALL.

 JUNE IS BUSTIN' OUT ALL OVER!

NETTIE.

 TO LADIES THE MEN ARE PAYIN' COURT.
 LOTSA SHIPS ARE KEPT AT ANCHOR
 JEST BECAUSE THE CAPTAINS HANKER
 FER A COMFORT THEY KEN ONLY GET IN PORT!

ALL.

 BECAUSE IT'S JUNE!

JUNE – JUNE – JUNE –
JEST BECAUSE IT'S JUNE – JUNE – JUNE!

NETTIE.

JUNE MAKES THE BAY LOOK BRIGHT AND NEW,
SAILS GLEAMIN' WHITE ON SUNLIT BLUE.

CARRIE.

JUNE IS BUSTIN' OUT ALL OVER,
THE OCEAN IS FULL OF JACKS AND JILLS.
WITH HER LITTLE TAIL A-SWISHIN'
EV'RY LADY FISH IS WISHIN'
THAT A MALE WOULD COME AND GRAB HER BY THE
    GILLS!

ALL.

JUNE IS BUSTIN' OUT ALL OVER!

NETTIE.

THE SHEEP AREN'T SLEEPIN' ANY MORE.
ALL THE RAMS THAT CHASE THE EWE SHEEP
ARE DETERMINED THERE'LL BE NEW SHEEP
AND THE EWE SHEEP AREN'T EVEN KEEPIN' SCORE!

ALL.

ON ACCOUNTA IT'S JUNE!
JUNE – JUNE – JUNE –
JEST BECAUSE IT'S JUNE – JUNE – JUNE!

[MUSIC NO. 08 "ENCORE: JUNE IS BUSTIN' OUT ALL OVER"]

JUNE IS BUSTIN' OUT ALL OVER!

NETTIE.

THE BEACHES ARE CROWDED EV'RY NIGHT.
FROM PENNOBSCOT TO AUGUSTY
ALL THE BOYS ARE FEELIN' LUSTY,
AND THE *GIRLS* AIN'T EVEN PUTTIN' UP A FIGHT.

(The **MEN** *begin to clear the baskets of clams as the* **FEMALE SINGERS** *settle in groups around the stage.)*

ALL.
BECAUSE IT'S JUNE!
JUNE – JUNE – JUNE –
JEST BECAUSE IT'S JUNE – JUNE – JUNE!

(On the last "June" one **GIRL** *begins to dance.* **OTHERS** *gradually join in.)*

[MUSIC NO. 09 "GIRLS' DANCE: JUNE IS BUSTIN' OUT ALL OVER"]

(The music becomes light-hearted and airy as the girls dance in celebration of this glorious June day. They welcome the warmth of the sun, opening themselves to all that nature has in store, as if experiencing everything for the first time. The **DANCERS** *seem to be pressing toward the sky, as do so many living things in June, on the verge of bursting into full bloom. After the dance all exit except* **NETTIE, CARRIE,** *and a small group of* **GIRLS.** **JULIE** *enters.)*

[MUSIC NO. 10 "JULIE'S ENTRANCE"]

CARRIE. Hello, Julie.

NETTIE. Did you find him?

JULIE. No. *(Explaining to* **CARRIE.***)* He went out with Jigger Craigin last night and he didn't come home.

CARRIE. Jigger Craigin?

JULIE. His new friend – he's a sailor on that big whaler, the *Nancy B.* She's sailing tomorrow. I'll be glad.

NETTIE. Why don't you two visit for a while.

(Necks are craned, ears cocked. **NETTIE** *notices this.)*

Look, girls, we got work to do. C'mon. You sweep those steps up there.

(Herding the **GIRLS** *upstage.)*

You set up there and keep outa the way and don't poke yer noses in other people's business.

JULIE. You need me, Cousin Nettie?

NETTIE. No. You stay out here and visit with Carrie. You haven't seen each other fer a long time. Do you good.

(She exits into the house. **JULIE** *and* **CARRIE** *sit on the bait box,* **JULIE** *right of* **CARRIE.** *All ears are open upstage.)*

CARRIE. Is he workin' yet?

JULIE. No. Nettie's been awful kind to us, lettin' us stay here with her.

CARRIE. Mr. Snow says a man that can't find work these days is jest bone lazy.

JULIE. Billy don't know any trade. He's only good at what he used to do. So now he jest don't do anythin'.

CARRIE. Wouldn't the carousel woman take him back?

JULIE. I think she would, but he won't go. I ask him why and he won't tell me... Last Monday he hit me.

CARRIE. Did you hit him back?

JULIE. No.

CARRIE. Whyn't you leave him?

JULIE. I don't want to.

CARRIE. I would. I'd leave him. Thinks he ken do whatever he likes jest because he's Billy Bigelow. Don't support you! Beats you...! He's a bad'n.

JULIE. He ain't willin'ly er meanin'ly bad.

CARRIE. *(Afraid she's hurting JULIE.)* Mebbe he ain't. That night you set on the bench together – he was gentle then, you told me.

JULIE. Yes, he was.

CARRIE. But now he's alw'ys actin' up...

JULIE. Not alw'ys. Sometimes he's gentle – even now. After supper, when he stands out here and listens to the music from the carousel – somethin' comes over him – and he's gentle.

CARRIE. What's he say?

JULIE. Nothin'. He jest sets and gets thoughtful. Y'see he's unhappy 'cause he ain't workin'. That's really why he hit me on Monday.

CARRIE. Fine reason fer hittin' you. Beats his wife 'cause he ain't workin'.

> *(She turns her head up left. GIRLS, caught eavesdropping, start to sweep vigorously.)*

JULIE. It preys on his mind.

CARRIE. Did he hurt you?

JULIE. *(Very eagerly.)* Oh, no – no.

CARRIE. Julie, I got some good news to tell you about me – about Mr. Snow and me. We're goin' to be cried in church nex' Sunday!

> *(The GIRLS who have been upstage turn quickly, come down and cluster around CARRIE, proving they haven't missed a thing. CARRIE rises.)*

ALL WOMEN. *(Ad libs of excitement.)* What's thet you say, Carrie...? Carrie...! Honest and truly...? You fixin' t'get hitched...? Well, I never...! Do tell...!

CARRIE. Jest a minute! Stop yer racket! Don't all come at me together!

(But she is really pleased.)

1ST WOMAN. Well, tell us! How long hev you been bespoke?

CARRIE. Near on t'two months. Julie was the fust t'know.

1ST WOMAN. What's he like, Julie?

CARRIE. Julie has never seen him. But you all will soon. He's comin' here. I asked him to the clambake.

1ST WOMAN. Can't hardly wait'll I see him.

2ND WOMAN. I can't hardly wait fer the weddin'.

(All look at each other and giggle.)

CARRIE. *(Giggling.)* Me neither.

JULIE. What a day that'll be fer ya!

[MUSIC NO. 11 "MISTER SNOW – REPRISE"]

WOMEN.
WHEN YOU WALK DOWN THE AISLE
ALL THE HEADS WILL TURN.
WHAT A RUSTLIN' OF BONNETS THERE'LL BE!
AND YOU'LL TRY TO SMILE,
BUT YOUR CHEEKS WILL BURN,
AND YOUR EYES'LL GET SO DIM, YOU KEN HARDLY SEE!
WITH YOUR ORANGE BLOSSOMS QUIVERIN' IN YOUR
HAND,
YOU WILL STUMBLE TO THE SPOT WHERE THE PARSON IS.
THEN YOUR FINGER WILL BE RINGED WITH A GOLDEN
BAND,
AND YOU'LL KNOW THE FELLER'S YOURS – AND YOU ARE
HIS.

CARRIE.
WHEN I MARRY MISTER SNOW –

WOMEN.

WHAT A DAY!

WHAT A DAY!

CARRIE.

THE FLOWERS'LL BE BUZZIN' WITH THE HUM OF BEES –

WOMEN.

THE BIRDS'LL MAKE A RACKET IN THE CHURCHYARD
TREES –

CARRIE.

WHEN I MARRY MISTER SNOW.

WOMEN.

HEIGH-HO!

CARRIE.

THEN IT'S OFF TO HOME WE'LL GO –

WOMEN.

SPILLIN' RICE

ON THE WAY!

CARRIE.

AND BOTH OF US'LL LOOK A LITTLE DREAMY-EYED,

A-DRIVIN' TO A COTTAGE BY THE OCEANSIDE

WHERE THE SALTY BREEZES BLOW –

(**ENOCH** *enters up left. He just couldn't be
anyone else.*)

WOMEN.

YOU AND MISTER SNOW!

(*Hearing his name,* **ENOCH** *preens.*)

CARRIE.

HE'LL CARRY ME 'CROSS THE THRESHOLD,

AND I'LL BE AS MEEK AS A LAMB.

THEN HE'LL SET ME ON MY FEET

AND I'LL SAY, KINDA SWEET:

(Spoken in rhythm.) "WELL, MISTER SNOW, HERE I AM!"

> *(Now* **ENOCH** *is very pleased. He makes his presence known by singing.)*

ENOCH.
THEN I'LL KISS HER SO SHE'LL KNOW –

CARRIE. *(Mortified.)*
MISTER SNOW!

WOMEN. *(Thrilled.)*
MISTER SNOW!

ENOCH.
THAT EVERYTHIN'LL BE AS RIGHT AS RIGHT KEN BE,
A-LIVIN' IN A COTTAGE BY THE SEA WITH ME,
WHERE THE SALTY BREEZES BLOW!

> *(**CARRIE** squeals and hides her head on* **JULIE***'s shoulder. The* **GIRLS** *are delighted.)*

I LOVE MISS PIPP'RIDGE AND I AIM TO
MAKE MISS PIPP'RIDGE CHANGE HER NAME TO
MISSUS ENOCH SNOW!

WOMEN. *(Ad libs.)* Carrie...! My lands, he give me sech a
start...! Well...! I never...!

CARRIE. *(Looking up at* **JULIE***.)* I'll never look him in the
face again! Never!

> *(Laughs, shouts, whoops, and squeals from the* **GIRLS***.)*

WOMEN. C'mon inside and leave the two love-birds alone!

> *(They exit into the house.* **CARRIE** *clings to* **JULIE** *and won't let her go.)*

CARRIE. *(Not turning to face him yet.)* Oh, Enoch!

ENOCH. Surprised?

CARRIE. Surprised? I'm mortified!

ENOCH. He-he!

> (*This, we are afraid, is the way he laughs.* **CARRIE** *straightens out, looks at him, then beams back at* **JULIE**.)

CARRIE. Well, this is him.

> (**ENOCH** *bows and smiles. There is a moment of awkward silence.*)

JULIE. Carrie told me a lot about you.

> (**CARRIE** *and* **JULIE** *nod to each other.* **CARRIE** *and* **ENOCH** *nod.*)

CARRIE. I told you a lot about Julie, didn't I?

> (**CARRIE** *and* **ENOCH** *nod.* **CARRIE** *and* **JULIE** *nod.*)

JULIE. Carrie tells me you're comin' to the clambake.

> (*He nods.*)

CARRIE. Looks like we'll hev good weather fer it, too.

> (*They nod.*)

JULIE. Not a cloud in the sky.

ENOCH. You're right.

CARRIE. (*To* **JULIE**.) He don't say much, but what he does say is awful pithy!

> (**JULIE** *nods.* **CARRIE** *looks over toward her love.*)

(*Still addressing* **JULIE**.) Is he anythin' like I told you he was?

JULIE. *Jest* like.

ENOCH. Oh, Carrie, I near fergot. I brought you some flowers.

CARRIE. *(Thrilled.)* Flowers? Where are they?

> (**ENOCH** *hands her a small envelope from his inside pocket. She reads what is written on the package.)*

Geranium seeds!

ENOCH. *(Handing her another envelope.)* And this'n here is hydrangea. Thought we might plant 'em in front of the cottage. *(To* **JULIE.***)* They do good in the salt air.

JULIE. That'll be beautiful!

ENOCH. I like diggin' around a garden in my spare time – like t'plant flowers and take keer o' them. Does your husband like that too?

JULIE. N-no. I couldn't rightly say if Billy likes to take *keer* of flowers. He likes t'smell 'em, though.

CARRIE. Enoch's nice lookin', ain't he?

ENOCH. Oh come, Carrie!

CARRIE. Stiddy and reliable too. Well, ain't you goin' to wish us luck?

JULIE. *(Warmly.)* Of course I wish you luck, Carrie.

> (**JULIE** *and* **CARRIE** *embrace.)*

CARRIE. You ken kiss Enoch, too – us bein' sech good friends, and me bein' right here lookin' at you.

> (**JULIE** *lets* **ENOCH** *kiss her on the cheek, which he shyly does. For a moment she clings to him, letting her head rest on this shoulder, as if it needed a shoulder very badly.* **JULIE** *starts to cry.)*

ENOCH. Why are you crying, Mrs... Er... Mrs...

CARRIE. It's because she has such a good heart.

ENOCH. We thank you for your heartfelt sympathy. We thank you Mrs... Er... Mrs...

JULIE. Mrs. Bigelow. Mrs. Billy Bigelow. That's my name – Mrs. B...

> *(She breaks off and starts to run into the house, but as she gets a little right of center, **BILLY** enters. He is followed by **JIGGER**. **JULIE** is embarrassed, recovers, and goes mechanically through the convention of introduction.)*

Billy, you know Carrie. This is her intended – Mr. Snow.

> *(**JIGGER** crosses up to the porch, standing under the arbor.)*

ENOCH. Mr. Bigelow! I almost feel like I know you.

BILLY. How are you?

> *(He starts up center.)*

ENOCH. I'm pretty well. Jest gettin' over a little chest cold.

> *(As **BILLY** gets up center.)*

This time of year – you know.

> *(He stops, seeing that **BILLY** isn't listening.)*

JULIE. *(Turning to **BILLY**.)* Billy!

BILLY. *(He stops and turns to **JULIE**, crosses down to her in a defiant manner.)* Well, all right, say it. I stayed out all night – and I ain't workin' – and I'm livin' off yer Cousin Nettie.

JULIE. I didn't say anything.

BILLY. No, but it was on the tip of yer tongue!

(He starts upstage center again.)

JULIE. Billy!

(He turns.)

Be sure and come back in time to go to the clambake.

BILLY. Ain't goin' to no clambake. Come on, Jigger.

> *(JIGGER, who has been slinking upstage out of
> the picture, joins BILLY and they exit upstage
> center and off left. JULIE stands watching
> them, turns to CARRIE, then darts into the
> house to hide her humiliation.)*

CARRIE. *(To ENOCH, after a pause.)* I'm glad you ain't got
no whoop-jamboree notions like Billy.

ENOCH. Well, Carrie, it alw'ys seemed t'me a man had
enough to worry about, gettin' a good sleep o' nights
so's to get in a good day's work the next day, without
goin' out an' lookin' fer any special trouble.

CARRIE. That's true, Enoch.

ENOCH. A man's got to make plans fer his life – and then
he's got to stick to 'em.

CARRIE. Your plans are turnin' out fine, ain't they, Enoch?

[MUSIC NO. 12 "WHEN THE CHILDREN ARE ASLEEP"]

ENOCH. All accordin' to schedule, so far.

I OWN A LITTLE HOUSE, AND I SAIL A LITTLE BOAT,
AND THE FISH I KETCH I SELL –
AND, IN A MANNER OF SPEAKIN',
I'M DOIN' VERY WELL.

I LOVE A LITTLE GIRL AND SHE'S IN LOVE WITH ME,
AND SOON SHE'LL BE MY BRIDE.
AND, IN A MANNER OF SPEAKIN',

I SHOULD BE SATISFIED.

CARRIE. *(Spoken in rhythm.)* WELL, AIN'T YOU?

ENOCH.

IF I TOLD YOU MY PLANS, AND THE THINGS I INTEND,
IT'D MAKE EV'RY CURL ON YER HEAD STAND ON END!

> *(He takes her hand and becomes more intense,
> the gleam of ambition coming into his eye.)*

WHEN I MAKE ENOUGH MONEY OUTA ONE LITTLE BOAT,
I'LL PUT ALL MY MONEY IN ANOTHER LITTLE BOAT.
I'LL MAKE TWIC'T AS MUCH OUTA TWO LITTLE BOATS,
AND THE FUST THING YOU KNOW I'LL HEV FOUR LITTLE
   BOATS!
THEN EIGHT LITTLE BOATS,
THEN A FLEET OF LITTLE BOATS!
THEN A GREAT BIG FLEET OF GREAT BIG BOATS!
ALL KETCHIN' HERRING,
BRINGIN' IT TO SHORE,
SAILIN' OUT AGAIN
AND BRINGIN' IN MORE,
AND MORE, AND MORE,
AND MORE!

> *(The music has become very operatic, rising
> in a crescendo far beyond what would
> ordinarily be justified by several boatloads of
> fish. But to this singer, boatloads of fish are
> kingdom come. The music continues under
> dialogue.)*

CARRIE. Who's goin' t'eat all thet herring?

ENOCH. They ain't goin' to *be* herring! Goin' to put 'em in cans and call 'em sardines. Goin' to build a little sardine cannery – then a big one – then the biggest one in the country. Carrie, I'm goin' to get rich on sardines. I mean *we're* goin' t'get rich – you and me. I mean you and me...and...all of us.

(CARRIE raises her eyes. Is the man bold
enough to be meaning "children"?)

THE FUST YEAR WE'RE MARRIED WE'LL HEV ONE LITTLE
KID,
THE SECOND YEAR WE'LL GO AND HEV ANOTHER LITTLE
KID.
YOU'LL SOON BE DARNIN' SOCKS FER EIGHT LITTLE
FEET –

CARRIE. *(Enough is enough.)*
ARE YOU BUILDIN' UP TO ANOTHER FLEET?

ENOCH. *(Blissfully proceeding with his dream.)*
WE'LL BUILD A LOT MORE ROOMS,
OUR DEAR LITTLE HOUSE'LL GET BIGGER,
OUR DEAR LITTLE HOUSE'LL GET BIGGER.

CARRIE. *(To herself.)*
AND SO WILL MY FIGGER!

(Music continues under dialogue.)

ENOCH. Carrie, ken y'imagine how it'll be when all the
kids are upstairs in bed, and you and me sit alone by
the fireside – me in my armchair, you on my knee –
mebbe?

CARRIE. Mebbe.

(And, to his great delight, CARRIE sits on his
knee. Both heave a deep, contented sigh, and
he starts to sing softly.)

ENOCH.
WHEN THE CHILDREN ARE ASLEEP, WE'LL SIT AND
DREAM
THE THINGS THAT EV'RY OTHER DAD AND MOTHER
DREAM.
WHEN THE CHILDREN ARE ASLEEP AND LIGHTS ARE LOW,
IF I STILL LOVE YOU THE WAY

I LOVE YOU TODAY,

YOU'LL PARDON MY SAYING, "I TOLD YOU SO!"

WHEN THE CHILDREN ARE ASLEEP, I'LL DREAM WITH
    YOU.

WE'LL THINK, "WHAT FUN WE HEV HAD!"

AND BE GLAD THAT IT ALL CAME TRUE.

CARRIE.

WHEN CHILDREN ARE AWAKE, A-ROMPIN' THROUGH THE
    ROOMS

OR RUNNIN' ON THE STAIRS,

THEN, IN A MANNER OF SPEAKIN',

THE HOUSE IS REALLY THEIRS.

BUT ONCE THEY CLOSE THEIR EYES AND WE ARE LEFT
    ALONE

AND FREE FROM ALL THEIR FUSS,

THEN, IN A MANNER OF SPEAKIN',

WE KEN BE REALLY US.

WHEN THE CHILDREN ARE ASLEEP, WE'LL SIT AND

ENOCH.

DREAM –   DREAM ALL ALONE –

THE THINGS THAT EV'RY OTHER DAD AND MOTHER

ENOCH.

DREAM.   DREAMS THAT WON'T BE
                            INTERRUPTED.

ENOCH.

WHEN THE CHILDREN ARE ASLEEP AND LIGHTS ARE

CARRIE.

LOW,   LO AND BEHOLD!

CARRIE.

IF I STILL LOVE YOU THE WAY

I LOVE YOU TODAY,

YOU'LL PARDON MY SAYING,

"I TOLD YOU SO!"

WHEN THE CHILDREN ARE ASLEEP, I'LL DREAM WITH

CARRIE.	ENOCH.
YOU.	YOU'LL DREAM WITH ME.

WE'LL THINK, "WHAT FUN WE HEV HAD!"
AND BE GLAD THAT IT ALL CAME TRUE!

ENOCH.

WHEN TODAY IS A LONG TIME AGO –

CARRIE & ENOCH.

YOU'LL STILL HEAR ME SAY THAT THE BEST DREAM I
KNOW IS –

ENOCH.	CARRIE.
YOU!	WHEN THE CHILDREN
	ARE ASLEEP, I'LL
	DREAM WITH YOU.

[MUSIC NO. 13 "BLOW HIGH, BLOW LOW"]

("Blow High, Blow Low" begins offstage.
ENOCH *looks off left, then up right, takes*
CARRIE*'s chin in his hands and kisses*
her gently on the forehead, as the **MEN** *–*
including the **DANCERS** *– enter singing, he*
looks up, takes his hat, which he left on the
bait box. Then he and **CARRIE** *exit.)*

MEN. *(Offstage.)*

BLOW HIGH, BLOW LOW!
A-WHALIN' WE WILL GO!
WE'LL GO A-WHALIN', A-SAILIN' AWAY.
AWAY WE'LL GO,
BLOW ME HIGH AND LOW!

*(***BILLY** *and* **JIGGER** *enter, followed by* **FRIENDS**
from **JIGGER***'s whaler.)*

FOR MANY AND MANY A LONG, LONG DAY!
FOR MANY AND MANY A LONG, LONG DAY!

(During the following refrain **BILLY** *looks*
toward the house. He is hesitant. Maybe

he should go in to **JULIE.** *He crosses center.* **JIGGER** *sees this, crosses over to* **BILLY.***)*

MEN. *(Very softly under dialogue.)*

BLOW HIGH, BLOW LOW! **JIGGER.** Hey, Billy!
A-WHALIN' WE WILL GO!

(**BILLY** *turns.*)

WE'LL GO A-WHALIN',   Where are you goin'?
A-SAILIN' AWAY.

(**BILLY** *looks indecisive.*)

AWAY WE'LL GO,   (**JIGGER** *takes his arm and brings him downstage.*)

BLOW ME HIGH   Stick with me. After we
AND LOW!   get rid of my shipmates, I wanna talk to you. Got an idea, for you and me to make money.

FOR MANY AND MANY   **BILLY.** How much?
A LONG, LONG DAY!   **JIGGER.** More'n you ever saw in yer life.

FOR MANY AND MANY   **A MAN.** Hey, Jigger, come
A LONG, LONG DAY!   back here!

LONG, LONG DAY!   (**BILLY** *and* **JIGGER** *go back to the boys.*)

JIGGER.
THE PEOPLE WHO LIVE ON LAND

ARE HARD TO UNDERSTAND –

WHEN YOU'RE LOOKIN' FOR FUN, THEY CLAP YOU INTO
    JAIL!

SO I'M SHIPPIN' OFF TO SEA,

WHERE LIFE IS GAY AND FREE,

AND A FELLER CAN FLIP

A HOOK IN THE HIP OF A WHALE.

ALL.

BLOW HIGH, BLOW LOW!

A-WHALIN' WE WILL GO!

WE'LL GO A-WHALIN', A-SAILIN' AWAY.

AWAY WE'LL GO,

BLOW ME HIGH AND LOW!

FOR MANY AND MANY A LONG, LONG DAY!

FOR MANY AND MANY A LONG, LONG DAY!

BILLY.

IT'S WONDERFUL JUST TO FEEL

YOUR HANDS UPON A WHEEL

AND TO LISTEN TO WIND A-WHISTIN' IN A SAIL!

OR TO CLIMB ALOFT AND BE

THE VERY FIRST TO SEE

A CHRYSANTHEMUM SPOUT

COME OUT O' THE SNOUT OF A WHALE!

ALL.

BLOW HIGH, BLOW LOW!

A-WHALIN' WE WILL GO!

WE'LL GO A-WHALIN', A-SAILIN' AWAY.

AWAY WE'LL GO,

BLOW ME HIGH AND LOW!

FOR MANY AND MANY A LONG, LONG DAY!

FOR MANY AND MANY A LONG, LONG DAY!

(**JIGGER** *draws* **BILLY** *and the* **MEN** *around
him. They go down to the footlights, crouch
low and* **JIGGER** *sings another verse.*)

JIGGER.

> A-ROCKIN' UPON THE SEA,
> YOUR BOAT WILL SEEM TO BE
> LIKE A DEAR LITTLE BABY IN HER BASSINET,
> FOR SHE HASN'T LEARNED TO WALK,
> AND SHE HASN'T LEARNED TO TALK,
> AND HER LITTLE BEHIND
> IS KIND OF INCLINED TO BE WET!

ALL.

> BLOW HIGH, BLOW LOW!
> A-WHALIN' WE WILL GO!
> WE'LL GO A-WHALIN', A-SAILIN' AWAY.
> AWAY WE'LL GO,
> BLOW ME HIGH AND LOW!
> FOR MANY AND MANY A LONG, LONG DAY!
> FOR MANY AND MANY A LONG, LONG DAY!

> *(The song ends, and the music segues into the "Hornpipe." As the* **MEN** *begin dancing,* **JIGGER** *takes* **BILLY** *off left.)*

[MUSIC NO. 14 "HORNPIPE"]

> *(***SAILORS** *and* **FISHERMEN** *start to dance a Hornpipe. The* **WOMEN** *try to get their attention and join the dance, but are ignored and snubbed by the* **MEN**.*)*

> *(The* **WOMEN** *wave their handkerchiefs and coquette with the* **MEN**, *but withdraw timidly. Both groups stand watching one another at opposite ends of the stage.)*

> *(At bar 115, the* **SAILORS** *and* **WOMEN** *ad lib taunts, urging* **HANNAH** *and the tallest* **SAILOR** *to dance together. These "ad libs" were indicated in the original published Vocal Score of* Carousel *but were not included in the*

*published libretto. Customers may use them
as a guide as desired.)*

1ST VOICE [MAN]. Thar she blows!

ALL MEN. H'ist yer mud 'ook!

2ND VOICE [MAN]. Spread you sails and get underway!

3RD VOICE [MAN]. Looks like a rowboat ridin' up to a
lighthouse!

4TH, 5TH, & 6TH VOICES [MEN]. Kidge!

Luff!

Scud!

7TH VOICE [WOMAN]. Go it, Hannah!

8TH VOICE [WOMAN]. Release your davits and jump!

9TH VOICE [WOMAN]. Keep afloat!

1ST VOICE [MAN]. Climb aloft!

*(The tallest **SAILOR** steps out of the group
to dance with **HANNAH**. After they dance,
the **MEN** leave. They run back to the sea.
The **WOMEN**, left deserted, wave forlornly.
HANNAH continues dancing in hope her
SAILOR will return. At the last moment, the
SAILOR returns and carries her off.)*

[MUSIC NO. 14A "HORNPIPE – EXIT"]

*(**BILLY** and **JIGGER** enter.)*

JIGGER. I tell you it's safe as sellin' cakes.

BILLY. You say this old sideburns who owns the mill is also
the owner of your ship?

JIGGER. That's right. And tonight he'll be takin' three or
four thousand dollars down to the captain – by hisself.

He'll walk along the waterfront by hisself – with all that money.

(*He pauses to let this sink in.*)

BILLY. You'd think he'd have somebody go with him.

JIGGER. Not him! Not the last three times, anyway. I watched him from the same spot and see him pass me. Once I nearly jumped him.

BILLY. Why didn't you?

JIGGER. Don't like to do a job 'less it's air-tight. This one needs two to pull it off proper. Besides, there was a moon – shinin' on him like a torch.

(*Spits.*)

Don't like moons.

(*This is good news.*)

Lately, the nights have been runnin' to fog. And it's ten to one we'll have fog tonight. That's why I wanted you to tell yer wife we'd go to that clambake.

BILLY. Clambake? Why?

JIGGER. Suppose we're all over on the island and you and me get lost in the fog for a half an hour. And suppose we got in a boat and come over here and...and did whatever we had to do, and then got back? There's yer alibi! We just say we were lost on the island all that time.

BILLY. Just what would we have to do? I mean me. What would *I* have to do?

JIGGER. You go up to old sideburns and say, "Excuse me, sir. Could you tell me the time?"

BILLY. "Excuse me, sir. Could you tell me the time?" Then what?

JIGGER. Then? Well, by that time I got my knife in his ribs. Then you take *your* knife...

BILLY. Me? I ain't got a knife.

JIGGER. You can get one, can't you?

BILLY. *(After a pause, turning to* **JIGGER.***)* Does he have to be killed?

JIGGER. No, he don't have to be. He can give up the money without bein' killed. But these New Englanders are funny. They'd rather be killed. Well?

BILLY. I won't do it! It's dirty.

JIGGER. What's dirty about it?

BILLY. The knife.

JIGGER. All right. Ferget the knife. Just go up to him with a tin cup and say, "Please, sir, will you give me three thousand dollars?" See what he does fer you.

BILLY. I ain't goin' to do it.

JIGGER. Of course, if you got all the money you want, and don't need...

BILLY. I ain't got a cent. Money thinks I'm dead.

> *(***MRS. MULLIN*** is seen entering from up left, unnoticed by* **BILLY** *and* **JIGGER.***)*

JIGGER. That's what I thought. And you're out of a job and you got a wife to support –

BILLY. Shut up about my wife.

> *(He sees* **MRS. MULLIN.***)*

What do you want?

MRS. MULLIN. Hello, Billy.

BILLY. What did you come fer?

MRS. MULLIN. Come to talk business.

JIGGER. Business!

(*He spits.*)

MRS. MULLIN. I see you're still hangin' around yer jailbird friend.

BILLY. What's it to you who I hang around with?

JIGGER. If there's one thing I can't abide, it's the common type of woman.

(*He saunters upstage left and stands looking out to sea.*)

BILLY. What are you doin' here? You got a new barker ain't you?

MRS. MULLIN. (*Looking him over.*) Whyn't you stay home and sleep at night? You look awful!

BILLY. He's as good as me, ain't he?

MRS. MULLIN. Push yer hair back off yer forehead...

BILLY. (*Pushing her hand away and turning away from her.*) Let my hair be.

MRS. MULLIN. If I told you to let it hang down over yer eyes you'd push it back. I hear you been beatin' her. If you're sick of her, why don't you leave her? No use beatin' the poor, skinny little...

BILLY. Leave her, eh? You'd like that, wouldn't you?

MRS. MULLIN. Don't flatter yourself!

(*Her pride stung, she paces to center stage.*)

If I had any sense I wouldn' of come here. The things you got to do when you're in business...! I'd sell the damn carousel if I could.

BILLY. Ain't it crowded without me?

MRS. MULLIN. Those fool girls keep askin' for you. They miss you, see? Are you goin' to be sensible and come back?

BILLY. And leave Julie?

MRS. MULLIN. You beat her, don't you?

BILLY. (*Exasperated.*) No, I don't beat her. What's all this damn-fool talk about beatin'? I hit her once, and now the whole town is... The next one I hear... I'll smash...

MRS. MULLIN. (*Backing away from him.*) All right! All right! I take it back. I don't want to get mixed up in it.

BILLY. Beatin' her! As if I'd beat her!

MRS. MULLIN. What's the odds one way er another? Look at the thing straight. You been married two months and you're sick of it. Out there's the carousel. Show booths, young girls, all the beer you want, a good livin' – and you're throwin' it all away. Know what? I got a new organ.

BILLY. I know.

MRS. MULLIN. How do you know?

BILLY. (*His voice softer.*) You can hear it from here. I listen to it every night.

MRS. MULLIN. Good one, ain't it?

BILLY. Jim dandy. Got a nice tone.

MRS. MULLIN. Y'ought to come up close and hear it. Makes you think the carousel is goin' faster. You belong out there and you know it. You ain't cut out fer a respectable married man. You're an artist type. You belong among artists. Tell you what – you come back and I'll give you a ruby ring my husband left me.

BILLY. I dunno – I might go back. I could still go on livin' here with Julie.

MRS. MULLIN. Holy Moses!

BILLY. What's wrong?

MRS. MULLIN. Can y'imagine how the girls'd love that? A barker who runs home to his wife every night! Why, people'd laugh theirselved sick.

BILLY. I know what *you* want.

MRS. MULLIN. Don't be so stuck on yerself.

BILLY. I ain't happy here, and *that's* the truth.

MRS. MULLIN. 'Course you ain't.

(*She strokes his hair back off his forehead, and this time he lets her.* JULIE *enters from house, carrying a tray with a cup of coffee and a plate of cakes on it.* MRS. MULLIN *pulls her hand away. There is a slight pause.*)

BILLY. Do you want anythin'?

JULIE. I brought you your coffee.

MRS. MULLIN. (*To* BILLY *in a low voice.*) Whyn't you have a talk with her? She'll understand. Maybe she'll be glad to get rid of you.

BILLY. (*Without conviction.*) Maybe.

JULIE. Billy – before I ferget. I got somethin' to tell you.

BILLY. All right.

JULIE. I been wantin' to tell you – in fact, I was goin' to yesterday.

BILLY. Well, go ahead.

JULIE. I can't – we got to be alone.

BILLY. Don't you see I'm busy? Here, I'm talkin' business and...

JULIE. It'll only take a minute.

BILLY. Get out o' here, or...

JULIE. I tell you it'll only take a minute.

BILLY. Will you get out of here?

JULIE. No.

BILLY. What did you say?

MRS. MULLIN.   Let her alone, Billy. I'll drop in at Bascombe's bank and get some small change for the carousel. I'll be back in a few minutes for your answer to my proposition.

> (*Exits above* JIGGER. *She looks at* JIGGER *as she goes.* JIGGER *looks at* BILLY, *then follows* MRS. MULLIN *off.*)

JULIE. Don't look at me like that. I ain't afraid of you – ain't afraid of anyone. I hev somethin' to tell you.

BILLY. Well then, tell me, and make it quick.

JULIE. I can't tell it so quick. Why don't you drink yer coffee?

BILLY. That what you wanted to tell me?

JULIE. No. By the time you drink it, I'll hev told you.

BILLY. (*Stirs coffee and takes a quick sip.*) Well?

JULIE. Yesterday my head ached and you asked me...

BILLY. Yes...

JULIE. Well – you see – thet's what it is.

BILLY. You sick?

JULIE. No. It's nothin' like thet.

> (*He puts cup down.*)

It's awful hard to tell you – I'm not a bit skeered, because it's a perfectly natural thing –

BILLY. What is?

JULIE. Well – when two people live together –

BILLY. Yes –

JULIE. I'm goin' to hev a baby.

> *(She turns away. He sits still and stunned. Then he rises, crosses to her, and puts his arms around her. She leans her head back on his shoulders. Then she leaves and starts for the house. As she goes to the steps,* **BILLY** *runs and helps her very solicitously.* **JIGGER** *has re-entered and calls to* **BILLY** *with two short whistles.)*

JIGGER. Hey, Billy!

BILLY. *(Turning to* **JIGGER.***)* Hey, Jigger! Julie... Julie's goin' to have a baby.

JIGGER. *(Calmly smoking his cigarette.)* Yeh? What about it?

BILLY. *(Disgusted at* **JIGGER.***)* Nothin'.

> *(He goes into the house.)*

JIGGER. *(Ruminating.)* My mother had a baby once.

> *(He smiles angelically and puffs on his cigarette.* **MRS. MULLIN** *enters.)*

MRS. MULLIN. He in there with her?

> *(***JIGGER** *ignores the question.)*

They're havin' it out, I bet.

> *(***JIGGER** *impudently blows a puff of smoke in her direction.)*

When he comes back to me I ain't goin' to let him hang around with you any more. You know that, don't you?

JIGGER. Common woman.

MRS. MULLIN. Ain't goin' to let him get in your clutches. Everybody that gets mixed up with you finishes in the jailhouse – or the grave.

JIGGER. Tut-tut-t-t-t. Carnival blonde! Comin' between a man and his wife!

MRS. MULLIN. Comin' between nothin'! They don't belong together. Nobody knows him like I do. And nobody is goin' to get him away from me. And that goes fer you!

JIGGER. Who wants him? If he's goin' to let himself get tied up to an old wobbly-hipped slut like you, what good would he be to me?

MRS. MULLIN. He won't be *no* good to you! And he won't end up with a perliceman's bullet in his heart – like that Roberts boy you hung around with last year. Wisht the bullet hadda got you – you sleek-eyed wharf rat! You keep away from him, that's all, or I'll get the cops after you.

JIGGER. *(Holding cigarette high.)* Common woman!

MRS. MULLIN. Yeh! Call names! But I got him back just the same! And you're through!

JIGGER. Put on a new coat o' paint. You're starting to peel! Old pleasure boat!

> *(He exits. She looks off after him, then turns right and sees **BILLY** coming out of the house. She immediately shifts her attention to the essential job of holding his interest. She primps and walks center. He comes down by bait box. A change has come over him. There is a strange, firm dignity in his manner.)*

BILLY. You still here?

> *(He picks up tray, and sits on box, tray in his lap.)*

MRS. MULLIN. Didn't you tell me to come back?

(Taking money out of dress.)

Here! You'll be wantin' an advance on yer salary. Well, that's only fair. You been out o' work a long time.

(She offers him money.)

BILLY. *(Taking another sip of coffee.)* Go home Mrs. Mullin.

MRS. MULLIN. What's the matter with you?

BILLY. Can't you see I'm havin' my breakfast? Go back to your carousel.

MRS. MULLIN. You mean you ain't comin' with me?

BILLY. *(Still holding cup.)* Get out of here. Get!

MRS. MULLIN. I'll never speak to you again – not if you were dyin', I wouldn't.

BILLY. That worries me a lot.

MRS. MULLIN. What did she tell you in there?

BILLY. *(Putting cup on tray.)* She told me...

MRS. MULLIN. Some lies about me, I bet!

BILLY. *(Proudly.)* No, Mrs. Mullin. Nothin' about you. Just about Julie and me – and...

(Looking up at her.)

As a matter of fact, Mrs. Mullin – I'm goin' to be a father!

MRS. MULLIN. You...! Julie...?

BILLY. Good-by, Mrs. Mullin.

MRS. MULLIN. You a father?

(She starts to laugh.)

BILLY. *(Giving her a good push.)* Get the hell away from here, Mrs. Mullin.

(She continues to laugh.)

Good-by, Mrs. Mullin!

[MUSIC NO. 15 "SOLILOQUY"]

*(He pushes her again, and as she reaches the
left portal, he gives her a good kick in the
bustle. Then he turns, looks toward* **NETTIE***'s
house, smiles. He starts to contemplate the
future. He starts to sing softly.)*

I WONDER WHAT HE'LL THINK OF ME!
I GUESS HE'LL CALL ME "THE OLD MAN."
I GUESS HE'LL THINK I CAN LICK
EV'RY OTHER FELLER'S FATHER –
WELL, I CAN!

(He gives his belt a hitch.)

I BET THAT HE'LL TURN OUT TO BE
THE SPIT AN' IMAGE
OF HIS DAD,
BUT HE'LL HAVE MORE COMMON SENSE
THAN HIS PUDDIN'-HEADED FATHER
EVER HAD.
I'LL TEACH HIM TO WRASSLE,
AND DIVE THROUGH A WAVE,
WHEN WE GO IN THE MORNIN'S FOR OUR SWIM.
HIS MOTHER CAN TEACH HIM
THE WAY TO BEHAVE,
BUT SHE WON'T MAKE A SISSY OUT O' HIM –
NOT HIM!
NOT MY BOY!
NOT BILL...

*(The name, coming to his lips involuntarily,
pleases him very much.)*

(Spoken in rhythm.) BILL!

(He loves saying it. He straightens up proudly.)

MY BOY, BILL!
I WILL SEE THAT HE'S NAMED
AFTER ME,
I WILL!
MY BOY, BILL –
HE'LL BE TALL.
AND AS TOUGH AS A TREE,
WILL BILL!

LIKE A TREE HE'LL GROW,
WITH HIS HEAD HELD HIGH
AND HIS FEET PLANTED FIRM ON THE GROUND,
AND YOU WON'T SEE NO –
BODY DARE TO TRY
TO BOSS HIM OR TOSS HIM AROUND!
NO POT-BELLIED, BAGGY-EYED BULLY'LL BOSS HIM
 AROUND!

(Having worked himself up to a high pitch of indignation, he relaxes into a more philosophical manner.)

I DON'T GIVE A DAMN WHAT HE DOES,
AS LONG AS HE DOES WHAT HE LIKES.
HE CAN SIT ON HIS TAIL
OR WORK ON A RAIL
WITH A HAMMER, A-HAMMERIN' SPIKES.
HE CAN FERRY A BOAT ON A RIVER
OR PEDDLE A PACK ON HIS BACK
OR WORK UP AND DOWN
THE STREETS OF A TOWN
WITH A WHIP AND A HORSE AND A HACK.

HE CAN HAUL A SCOW ALONG A CANAL,
RUN A COW AROUND A CORRAL,
OR MAYBE BARK FOR A CAROUSEL –

(This worries him.)

OF COURSE IT TAKES TALENT TO DO *THAT* WELL.

HE MIGHT BE A CHAMP OF THE HEAVYWEIGHTS
OR A FELLER THAT SELLS YOU GLUE,
OR PRESIDENT OF THE UNITED STATES –
THAT'D BE ALL RIGHT, TOO.

> *(Orchestra picks up the theme of "My boy,
> Bill." **BILLY** speaks over music.)*

His mother'd like that. But he wouldn't be President
unless he wanted to be!

NOT BILL!
MY BOY, BILL –
HE'LL BE TALL.
AND AS TOUGH AS A TREE,
WILL BILL!
LIKE A TREE HE'LL GROW
WITH HIS HEAD HELD HIGH,
AND HIS FEET PLANTED FIRM ON THE GROUND,
AND YOU WON'T SEE NO –
BODY DARE TO TRY
TO BOSS HIM OR TOSS HIM AROUND!
NO FAT-BOTTOMED, FLABBY-FACE, POT-BELLIED, BAGGY-
    EYED BASTARD'LL BOSS HIM AROUND!

> *(He paces the stage angrily.)*

AND I'M DAMNED IF HE'LL MARRY HIS BOSS'S DAUGHTER,
A SKINNY-LIPPED VIRGIN WITH BLOOD LIKE WATER,
WHO'LL GIVE HIM A PECK AND CALL IT A KISS
AND LOOK IN HIS EYES THROUGH A LORGNETTE...

(Spoken in rhythm.) SAY! WHY AM I TAKIN' ON LIKE THIS?
(Sung.) MY KID AIN'T EVEN BEEN BORN YET!

> *(He laughs loudly at himself, crosses up to
> bait box, and sits. Then he returns to more
> agreeable daydreaming.)*

I CAN SEE HIM
WHEN HE'S SEVENTEEN OR SO
AND STARTIN' IN TO GO
WITH A GIRL!
I CAN GIVE HIM
LOTS O' POINTERS, VERY SOUND,
ON THE WAY TO GET ROUND
ANY GIRL.
I CAN TELL HIM –

(Spoken in rhythm.) WAIT A MINUTE! COULD IT BE?
WHAT THE HELL! WHAT IF HE IS A GIRL!

> *(Rises in anguish.)*

Bill! Oh, Bill...!

> *(He sits on bait box and holds his head in his*
> *hands. The music becomes the original theme*
> *"I wonder what he'll think of me." He speaks*
> *over it in a moaning voice.)*

What would I do with her? What could I do *for* her? A
bum – with no money!

YOU CAN HAVE FUN WITH A SON,
BUT YOU GOT TO BE A FATHER
TO A GIRL!

> *(Thinking it over, he begins to be reconciled.)*

SHE MIGHTN'T BE SO BAD AT THAT –
A KID WITH RIBBONS IN HER HAIR!
A KIND O' SWEET AND PETITE
LITTLE TINTYPE OF HER MOTHER –
WHAT A PAIR!

I can just hear myself braggin' about her!

> *(In the original Broadway production the*
> *lyrics from "When I have a daughter" to*
> *"Things that I always say" were omitted; if*

*the licensee chooses to do that, also omit the
line "I can just hear myself braggin' about
her!")*

WHEN I HAVE A DAUGHTER,
I'LL STAND AROUND IN BARROOMS,
OH, HOW I'LL BOAST AND BLOW!
FRIENDS'LL SEE ME COMIN'
AND EMPTY ALL THE BARROOMS,
THROUGH EV'RY DOOR THEY'LL GO,
WEARY OF HEARIN' DAY AFTER DAY,
THE SAME OLD THINGS THAT I ALWAYS SAY...
MY LITTLE GIRL,
SWEET AND LIGHT
AS PEACHES AND CREAM IS SHE.
MY LITTLE GIRL
IS HALF AGAIN AS BRIGHT
AS GIRLS ARE MEANT TO BE!
DOZENS OF BOYS PURSUE HER,
MANY A LIKELY LAD
DOES WHAT HE CAN TO WOO HER
FROM HER FAITHFUL DAD.
SHE HAS A FEW
SWEET AND LIGHT
YOUNG FELLERS OF TWO OR THREE –
BUT MY LITTLE GIRL
GETS HUNGRY EV'RY NIGHT
AND SHE COMES HOME TO ME...

My little girl!

(More thoughtful, and serious.)

My little girl!

(Suddenly panicky.)

I GOT TO GET READY BEFORE SHE COMES,

I GOT TO MAKE CERTAIN THAT SHE
WON'T BE DRAGGED UP IN SLUMS
WITH A LOT O' BUMS –
LIKE ME!
SHE'S GOT TO BE SHELTERED AND FED, AND DRESSED
IN THE BEST THAT MONEY CAN BUY!
I NEVER KNEW HOW TO GET MONEY,
BUT I'LL TRY –
BY GOD! I'LL TRY!
I'LL GO OUT AND MAKE IT,
OR STEAL IT, OR TAKE IT
OR DIE!

> *(Finishing, he stands still and thoughtful.
> Then he turns right and walks slowly up to
> the bait box and gazes off right. As he does,*
> **NETTIE** *comes out of the house, carrying a
> large jug.)*

[MUSIC NO. 16 "FINALE ACT I"]

> *(She crosses up center and puts the jug on the
> steps left center, then calls off.)*

NETTIE. Hey, you roustabouts! Time to get goin'! Come and help us carry everythin' on the boats!

1ST MAN. *(Offstage.)* All right, Nettie, we're comin'!

2ND MAN. Don't need to hev a fit about it.

NETTIE. Hey, Billy! What's this Julie says about you not goin' to the clambake?

BILLY. Clambake?

> *(Suddenly getting an idea from the word.)*

Mebbe I *will* go, after all!

> *(General laughter offstage.* **JIGGER** *enters
> down left.* **BILLY** *sees him.)*

(To **NETTIE.***)* There's Jigger. I got to talk to him. Jigger!
Hey, Jigger! Come here – quick!

NETTIE. I'll tell Julie you're comin'. She'll be tickled pink.

(She goes into the house.)

BILLY. Jigger, I changed my mind! You know – about goin'
to the clambake, and... I'll do everythin' like you said.
Gotta get money on account of the baby, see.

JIGGER. Sure, the baby!

(He pulls **BILLY** *closer and lowers his voice.)*

Did you get the knife?

BILLY. Knife?

JIGGER. I only got a pocket knife. If he shows fight we'll
need a real one.

BILLY. But I ain't got...

JIGGER. Go inside and take the kitchen knife.

BILLY. Somebody might see me.

JIGGER. Take it so they don't see you!

*(***BILLY** *looks indecisive.* **JULIE** *enters on the
run to* **BILLY** *from the house.)*

JULIE. Billy, is it true? Are you comin' to the clambake?

BILLY. I think so. Yes.

*(Puts her arm around his waist. He puts his
arms around her.)*

JULIE. We'll hev a barrel of fun. I'll show you all over the
island. Know every inch of it. Been goin' to picnics
there since I been a little girl.

JIGGER. Billy! Billy! Y'better go and get that...

JULIE. Get what, Billy?

BILLY. Why...

JIGGER. The shawl. Billy said you oughter have a shawl. Gets cold at nights. Fog comes up – ain't that what you said?

> (**PEOPLE** *start entering with baskets, pies, jugs, etc., ready to go to the clambake.*)

BILLY. Y-yes. I better go and get it – the shawl.

JULIE. Now, that was real thoughtful, Billy.

> (*We see* **NETTIE** *coming out of the house. The stage is pretty well crowded by now.*)

BILLY. I'll go and get it.

> (*He exits into the house quickly.*)

NETTIE. C'mon, all!

> (*From the house come girls carrying cakes, pies, butter crocks;* **MEN** *carrying baskets.*)

JUNE IS BUSTIN' OUT ALL OVER!

WOMEN.
THE FLOWERS ARE BUSTIN' FROM THEIR SEED!

NETTIE.
AND THE PLEASANT LIFE OF RILEY,
THAT IS SPOKEN OF SO HIGHLY,
IS THE LIFE THAT EV'RYBODY WANTS TO LEAD!

ALL.
BECAUSE IT'S JUNE!
JUNE – JUNE – JUNE!
JEST BECAUSE IT'S JUNE – JUNE – JUNE!
BECAUSE IT'S JUNE!
BECAUSE IT'S JUNE!
BECAUSE IT'S JUNE!
BECAUSE IT'S JUNE!

*(During this singing chorus, **ENOCH** and **CARRIE** have entered from the house. **JULIE** is seen running over to **CARRIE** to tell her the good news that **BILLY** is going to the clambake. **JIGGER** crosses to **JULIE** and is introduced to **CARRIE**. **JIGGER** looks her over. **JULIE** also introduces **JIGGER** to **ENOCH**, but **JIGGER** just brushes him off. **ENOCH** tries to smile, but misses by a good margin. On the last "June" of the refrain, everyone but **JULIE** and **JIGGER** has exited. **BILLY** comes out of the house carrying the shawl. He crosses to **JULIE**, who is now a little left of center and downstage. **JIGGER** is right stage. As **BILLY** is putting the shawl over **JULIE**'s shoulder, **JIGGER** works his way over to **BILLY** as if to say, "Did you get the knife?" **BILLY** pantomimes that it's in the inside pocket of his vest. **JULIE** turns in time to see this. **BILLY** quickly takes her arm and walks her off. **JIGGER** has his pocket knife in his hand and is testing the sharpness of the blade and is following **BILLY** off as...)*

The Curtain Falls

ACT II

[MUSIC NO. 17 "ENTR'ACTE"]

Scene One:
On An Island Across The Bay, That Night

[MUSIC NO. 18 "OPENING ACT II"]

(The backdrop depicts the bay, seen between two sand dunes. It is too dark to define the characters until a moment after the rise of the curtain when the lights start a gradual "dim up," as if a cloud were unveiling the moon. Down left **BILLY** *is seen lying stretched at full length, his head on* **JULIE***'s lap. There is a small group right center dominated by* **NETTIE, ENOCH,** *and* **CARRIE.** *Upstage several couples recline in chosen isolation at the edge of the trees. The mood of the scene is the languorous contentment that comes to people who have just had a good meal in the open air. The curtain is up several seconds before a groaning sigh rolls like a wave through the entire crowd.)*

NETTIE. Dunno as I should hev et those last four dozen clams!

A GIRL. Look here, Orrin Peasely! You jest keep your hands in yer pockets if they're so cold.

[MUSIC NO. 19 "A REAL NICE CLAMBAKE"]

ALL. *(Softly.)*

THIS WAS A REAL NICE CLAMBAKE,
WE'RE MIGHTY GLAD WE CAME.
THE VITTLES WE ET
WERE GOOD, YOU BET!
THE COMPANY WAS THE SAME.
OUR HEARTS ARE WARM,
OUR BELLIES ARE FULL,
AND WE ARE FEELIN' PRIME.
THIS WAS A REAL NICE CLAMBAKE,
AND WE ALL HAD A REAL GOOD TIME!

NETTIE.

FUST COME CODFISH CHOWDER,
COOKED IN IRON KETTLES,
ONIONS FLOATIN' ON THE TOP,
CURLIN' UP IN PETALS!

JULIE.

THROWED IN RIBBONS OF SALTED PORK –

MEN.

AN OLD NEW ENGLAND TRICK!

JULIE.

AND LAPPED IT ALL UP WITH A CLAMSHELL,
TIED ONTO A BAYBERRY STICK!

ALL.

OH...
THIS WAS A REAL NICE CLAMBAKE,
WE'RE MIGHTY GLAD WE CAME.
THE VITTLES WE ET
WERE GOOD, YOU BET!
THE COMPANY WAS THE SAME.
OUR HEARTS ARE WARM,
OUR BELLIES ARE FULL,
AND WE ARE FEELIN' PRIME.
THIS WAS A REAL NICE CLAMBAKE,

AND WE ALL HAD A REAL GOOD TIME!

> *(The memory of the delectable feast restores* **ENOCH***'s spirit and he rises and crosses to center and sings very soulfully.)*

ENOCH.
REMEMBER WHEN WE RAKED
THEM RED-HOT LOBSTERS
OUT OF THE DRIFTWOOD FIRE?
THEY SIZZLED AND CRACKLED
AND SPUTTERED A SONG
FITTEN FOR AN ANGELS' CHOIR.

WOMEN. *(Whisper.)*
FITTEN FER AN ANGELS',
FITTEN FER AN ANGELS',
FITTEN FER AN ANGELS' CHOIR!

NETTIE.
WE SLIT 'EM DOWN THE BACK
AND PEPPERED 'EM GOOD,
AND DOUSED 'EM IN MELTED BUTTER –

CARRIE. *(Savagely.)*
THEN WE TORE AWAY THE CLAWS
AND CRACKED 'EM WITH OUR TEETH
'CAUSE WE WEREN'T IN THE MOOD TO PUTTER!

WOMEN. *(Whisper.)*
FITTEN FER AN ANGELS',
FITTEN FER AN ANGELS',
FITTEN FER AN ANGELS' CHOIR!

A MAN (BARITONE SOLO).
THEN, AT LAST, COME THE CLAMS –

ALL MEN.
STEAMED UNDER ROCKWEED
AN' POPPIN' FROM THEIR SHELLS –

ALL.

> JEST HOW MANY OF 'EM
> GALLOPED DOWN OUR GULLETS –
> WE COULDN'T SAY OURSEL'S!
>
> OH...
> THIS WAS A REAL NICE CLAMBAKE,
> WE'RE MIGHTY GLAD WE CAME.
> THE VITTLES WE ET
> WERE GOOD, YOU BET!
> THE COMPANY WAS THE SAME.
> OUR HEARTS ARE WARM,
> OUR BELLIES ARE FULL,
> AND WE ARE FEELIN' PRIME!
> THIS WAS A REAL NICE CLAMBAKE,
> AND WE ALL HAD A REAL GOOD TIME!
>
> WE SAID IT AFORE AND WE'LL SAY IT AGEN –
> WE ALL HAD A REAL GOOD TIME!

CARRIE. Hey, Nettie! Ain't it 'bout time the boys started their treasure hunt?

MEN. *(Ad libs.)* Sure...! Feel like I'm goin' to win this year...! Let's get goin' ...!

NETTIE. Jest a minute! Nobody's goin' treasure huntin' till we get this island cleaned up. Can't leave it like this fer the next picnickers that come.

MEN. Ah, Nettie...

NETTIE. Bogue in and get to work! The whole kit and kaboodle of you! Burn that rubbish! Gather up those bottles!

ALL. *(Ad libs.)* All right, all right... Needn't hev a catnip fit...!

> (**JULIE** *exits. All start to leave the stage in all directions.*)

NETTIE. Hey, Enoch! While they're cleanin' up, you go hide the treasure.

(She exits.)

JIGGER. Why should *he* get out of workin'?

CARRIE. *(Proudly.)* 'Cause he found the treasure last year. One that finds it hides it the next year. That's the way we do!

> *(CARRIE and ENOCH cross upstage of BILLY and JIGGER and exit. JIGGER starts to follow.)*

BILLY. Hey, Jigger!

JIGGER. *(Looking off after CARRIE.)* That's a well-set-up little piece, that Carrie.

BILLY. Ain't it near time fer us to start?

JIGGER. No. We'll wait till they're ready fer that treasure hunt. That'll be a good way fer you and me to leave. We'll be a team, see? Then we'll get lost together like I said.

> *(BILLY is moving about nervously.)*

Stop jumping from one foot to the other. Go along to yer wife – and tell that little Carrie to come and talk to me.

BILLY. Look, Jigger, you ain't got time fer girls tonight.

JIGGER. Sure I have. You know me – quick or nothin'!

BILLY. Jigger – after we do it – what do we do then?

JIGGER. Bury the money – and go on like nothin' happened for six months. Wait another six months and then buy passage on a ship.

BILLY. The baby'll be born by then.

JIGGER. We'll take it along with us.

BILLY. Maybe we'll sail to San Francisco.

JIGGER. Why do you keep puttin' yer hand on yer chest?

BILLY. My heart's jumpin' up and down under the knife.

JIGGER. Put the knife on the other side.

>   (CARRIE *enters.*)

CARRIE. Mr. Bigelow, Julie says you should come and help her.

>   (BILLY *exits.* CARRIE *turns to* JIGGER.)

JIGGER. I don't feel so well.

CARRIE. It's mebbe the clams not settin' so good on yer stummick.

JIGGER. Nope. It's nothin' on my stummick. It's somethin' on my mind.

>   (*He takes* CARRIE's *arm.*)

Sit down here with me a minute. I want yer advice.

CARRIE. (*Sitting on an upturned basket.*) Now, look here, Mr. Craigin, I ain't got no time fer no wharf yarns or spoondrift.

JIGGER. (*Squashing out his cigarette.*) I want yer advice.

>   (*Suddenly throws his arms around her.*)

You're sweeter than sugar and I'm crazy fer you. Never had this feelin' before fer anyone –

CARRIE. Mr. Craigin!

JIGGER. Ain't nothin' I wouldn't do fer you. Why, jest to see yer lovely smile – I'd swim through beer with my mouth closed. You're the only girl fer me. How about a little kiss?

CARRIE. Mr. Craigin, I couldn't.

JIGGER. Didn't you hear me say I loved you?

CARRIE. I'm awful sorry for you, but what can I do? Enoch and me are goin' to be cried in church next Sunday.

JIGGER. Next Sunday I'll be far out at sea lookin' at the icy gray water. Mebbe I'll jump in and drown myself!

CARRIE. Oh, don't!

JIGGER. Well, then, give me a kiss.

(*Grabbing her arm. Good and sore now.*)

One measly little kiss!

CARRIE. (*Pushing his arm away.*) Enoch wouldn't like it.

JIGGER. I don't wanta kiss Enoch.

CARRIE. (*Drawing herself up resolutely.*) I'll thank you not to yell at me, Mr. Craigin. If you love me like you say you do, then please show me the same respect like you would if you didn't love me.

(*She starts to stalk off left.* **JIGGER** *is a stayer and not easily shaken off. He decides to try one more method. It worked once long ago on a girl in Liverpool.*)

JIGGER. (*In despair.*) Carrie!

(*She stops; he crosses to her.*)

Miss Pipperidge! Just one word, please.

(*He becomes quite humble.*)

I know I don't deserve yer fergiveness. Only, I couldn't help myself. Fer a few awful minutes I... I let the brute come out in me.

CARRIE. I think I understand, Mr. Craigin.

JIGGER. Thank you, Miss Pipperidge, thank you kindly. There's just one thing that worries me and it worries me a lot – it's about you.

CARRIE. About me?

JIGGER. You're such a little innercent. You had no right to stay here alone and talk with a man you hardly knew.

Suppose I was a different type of feller – you know, unprincipled – a feller who'd use his physical strength to have his will. There are such men, you know.

CARRIE. I know, but...

JIGGER. Every girl ought to know how to defend herself against beasts like that. (*Proceeding slyly up to his point.*) Now, there are certain grips in wrestlin' I could teach you – tricks that'll land a masher flat on his face in two minutes.

CARRIE. But I ain't strong enough –

JIGGER. It don't take strength – it's all in balance – a twist of the wrist and a dig with the elbow. Here, just let me show you a simple one. This might save yer life some day. Suppose a feller grabs you like this.

(*Puts both arms around her waist.*)

Now you put yer two hands on my neck.

(*She does.*)

Now pull me toward you.

(*She does.*)

That's it. Now pull my head down. Good! Now put yer left arm all the way around my neck. Now squeeze – hard! Tighter!

(*Slides his right hand down her back and pats her bustle.*)

Good girl!

CARRIE. (*Holding him tight.*) Does it hurt?

JIGGER. (*Having the time of his life.*) You got me helpless!

CARRIE. Show me another one!

(*She lets him go.*)

JIGGER. Right! Here's how you can pick a feller up and send him sprawlin'. Now I'll stand here, and you get hold of... Wait a minute. I'll do it to you first. Then you can do it to me. Stand still and relax.

> *(He takes her hand and foot and slings her quickly over his shoulders.)*

This is the way firemen carry people.

CARRIE. *(A little breathless and stunned.)* Is it?

JIGGER. See how helpless you can make a feller if he gets fresh with you?

> *(He starts to walk off with her.)*

CARRIE. Mr. Craig...

> *(She stops, because something terrible has happened. ENOCH has entered. JIGGER sees him and stops, still holding CARRIE over his shoulders, fireman style. After a terrifying pause, CARRIE speaks.)*

Hello, Enoch.

> *(No answer.)*

This is the way firemen carry people.

ENOCH. *(Grimly.)* Where's the fire?

> *(JIGGER puts her down between ENOCH and himself.)*

CARRIE. *(Crossing to ENOCH.)* He was only showin' me how to defend myself.

ENOCH. It didn't look like you had learned very much by the time I came!

JIGGER. Oh, what's all the fussin' and fuzzlin' and wuzzlin' about?

ENOCH. In my opinion, sir, you are as scurvy a hunk o' scum as I ever see near the water's edge at low tide!

JIGGER. *(Turning his profile to* **ENOCH**.*)* The same – side view!

ENOCH. I – I never thought I'd see the woman I am engaged to bein' carried out o' the woods like a fallen deer!

CARRIE. He wasn't carryin' me out o' the woods. He was carryin' me *into* the woods. No, I don't mean that!

ENOCH. I think we hev said all we hev to say. I can't abide women who are free, loose, and lallygaggin' – and I certainly would never marry one.

CARRIE. But, Enoch!

ENOCH. Leave me, please. Leave me alone with my shattered dreams. They are all I hev left – memories of what didn't happen!

> **[MUSIC NO. 20 "GERANIUMS IN THE WINDER" & "STONECUTTERS CUT IT ON STONE"]**
>
> (**CARRIE** *turns upstage and crosses to* **JIGGER**. *He puts his arms around her. She starts to whimper.* **ENOCH** *looks out into space with pained eyes, and sings broad and emphatically.*)

GERANIUMS IN THE WINDER,
HYDRANGEAS ON THE LAWN,
AND BREAKFAST IN THE KITCHEN
IN THE TIMID PINK OF DAWN,
AND YOU TO BLOW ME KISSES
WHEN I HEADED FER THE SEA –
WE MIGHT HEV BEEN
A HAPPY PAIR
OF LOVERS –
MIGHTN'T HEV WE?

(Another sob from **CARRIE**.*)*

AND COMIN' HOME AT TWILIGHT,
IT MIGHT HEV BEEN SO SWEET
TO TAKE MY KETCH OF HERRING
AND LAY THEM AT YOUR FEET!

(Swallowing hard.)

I MIGHT HEV HED A BABY –

JIGGER. *(Spoken in rhythm.)* WHAT?!

ENOCH. *(Glares at* **JIGGER**, *then out front again.)*
TO DANDLE ON MY KNEE,
BUT ALL THESE THINGS
THAT MIGHT HEV BEEN,
ARE NEVER,
NEVER TO BE!

(At this point **CARRIE** *just lets loose and bawls, and buries her head in* **JIGGER**'s *shoulder. Some people hear this and enter as* **JIGGER** *consoles her.)*

JIGGER.
I NEVER SEE IT YET TO FAIL,
I NEVER SEE IT FAIL!
A GIRL WHO'S IN LOVE WITH A VIRTUOUS MAN
IS DOOMED TO WEEP AND WAIL.

(More people enter and get into the scene.)

STONECUTTERS CUT IT ON STONE,
WOODPECKERS PECK IT ON WOOD:
THERE'S NOTHIN' SO BAD FER A WOMAN
AS A MAN WHO THINKS HE'S GOOD!

*(**CARRIE** bawls out one loud note. More people enter, **NETTIE** is with them.)*

ENOCH. Nice talk!

JIGGER.
> MY MOTHER USED TO SAY TO ME,
> "WHEN YOU GROW UP, MY SON,
> I HOPE YOU'RE A BUM LIKE YER FATHER WAS,
> 'CAUSE A GOOD MAN AIN'T NO FUN."

JIGGER & CHORUS.
> STONECUTTERS CUT IT ON STONE,
> WOODPECKERS PECK IT ON WOOD:
> THERE'S NOTHIN' SO BAD FER A WOMAN
> AS A MAN WHO THINKS HE'S GOOD!

> *(From here on, the* **CHORUS** *takes sides.)*

ENOCH.
> 'TAIN'T SO!

JIGGER.
> 'TIS TOO!

ENOCH'S CHORUS.
> 'TAIN'T SO!

JIGGER'S CHORUS.
> 'TIS TOO!

> *(***ENOCH** *crosses to right, followed by* **CARRIE***.)*

CARRIE. Enoch – say you forgive me! Say somethin' sweet to me, Enoch – somethin' soft and sweet.

> *(He remains silent and she becomes exasperated.)*

Say somethin' soft and sweet!

ENOCH. *(Turning to* **CARRIE***, fiercely.)* Boston cream pie!

> *(He turns and exits.* **CARRIE** *cries.* **BILLY** *enters and crosses to* **JIGGER***.)*

BILLY. Hey, Jigger – don't you think?

JIGGER. Huh? *(Catches on, raises his voice to all.)* When are we goin' to start that treasure hunt?

NETTIE. Right now! Y'all got yer partners? Two men to each team. You got half an hour to find the treasure. The winners can kiss any girls they want!

> *(A whoop and a holler goes up and all the* **MEN** *and the* **DANCING** *girls start out.* **JULIE** *enters from down left and sees* **BILLY** *starting out with* **JIGGER***.)*

JULIE. Billy – are you goin' with Jigger? Don't you think that's foolish?

BILLY. Why?

JULIE. Neither one of you knows the island good. You ought to split up and each go with –

BILLY. *(Brushing her aside.)* We're partners, see? C'mon, Jigger.

CARRIE. I don't know what gets into men. Enoch put on a new suit today and he was a different person.

> *(They all group around* **JULIE***.)*

1ST WOMAN.
I NEVER SEE IT YET TO FAIL.

ALL WOMEN.
I NEVER SEE IT FAIL.
A GIRL WHO'S IN LOVE WITH ANY MAN
IS DOOMED TO WEEP AND WAIL.

1ST WOMAN. And it's even worse after they marry you.

2ND WOMAN. You ought to give him back that ring, Carrie. You'd be better off.

3RD WOMAN. Here's Arminy* – been married a year. She'll tell you!

---

* Pronounced Ar-MINE-y.

ARMINY. *(Singing with a feeling of futility.)*
    THE CLOCK JEST TICKS YER LIFE AWAY,
    THERE'S NO RELIEF IN SIGHT.
    IT'S COOKIN' AND SCRUBBIN' AND SEWIN' ALL DAY,
    AND GAWD-KNOWS-WHATIN' ALL NIGHT!

ALL WOMEN.
    STONECUTTERS CUT IT ON STONE,
    WOODPECKERS PECK IT ON WOOD:
    THERE'S NOTHIN' SO BAD FER A WOMAN
    AS A MAN WHO'S BAD OR GOOD!

CARRIE. It makes you wonder, don't it?

1ST WOMAN. Now you tell her, Julie.

2ND WOMAN. She's your best girlfriend.

[MUSIC NO. 21 "WHAT'S THE USE OF WOND'RIN'?"]

ALL WOMEN. *(Spoken in rhythm.)* TELL IT TO HER
GOOD, JULIE,
    TELL IT TO HER GOOD!

      *(**JULIE** smiles as the **GIRLS** group surround her
      expectantly. **JULIE** starts singing softly and
      earnestly to **CARRIE**, but as she goes on, she
      quite obviously becomes autobiographical in
      her philosophy. Her singing is quiet, almost
      recited. The orchestration is light. The **GIRLS**
      hold the picture, perfectly still, like figures in
      a painting.)*

JULIE. *(Softly and earnestly.)*
    WHAT'S THE USE OF WOND'RIN'
    IF HE'S GOOD OR IF HE'S BAD,
    OR IF YOU LIKE THE WAY HE WEARS HIS HAT?
    OH, WHAT'S THE USE OF WOND'RIN'
    IF HE' S GOOD OR IF HE'S BAD?
    HE'S YOUR FELLER AND YOU LOVE HIM –

THAT'S ALL THERE IS TO THAT.

COMMON SENSE MAY TELL YOU
THAT THE ENDIN' WILL BE SAD
AND NOW'S THE TIME TO BREAK AND RUN AWAY.
BUT WHAT' THE USE OF WOND'RIN'
IF THE ENDIN' WILL BE SAD?
HE'S YOUR FELLER AND YOU LOVE HIM –
THERE'S NOTHIN' MORE TO SAY.

SOMETHIN' MADE HIM THE WAY THAT HE IS,
WHETHER HE'S FALSE OR TRUE.
AND SOMETHIN' GAVE HIM THE THINGS THAT ARE HIS –
ONE OF THOSE THINGS IS YOU.

SO, WHEN HE WANTS YOUR KISSES
YOU WILL GIVE THEM TO THE LAD,
AND ANYWHERE HE LEADS YOU, YOU WILL WALK.
AND ANYTIME HE NEEDS YOU,
YOU'LL GO RUNNIN' THERE LIKE MAD!
YOU'RE HIS GIRL AND HE'S YOUR FELLER –
AND ALL THE REST IS TALK.

> (As **JULIE** *finishes her song, we see* **BILLY** *and* **JIGGER** *entering, crouching behind the sand dunes.* **JULIE** *turns just in time to see them as they get up center.* **JULIE** *crosses to* **BILLY**.)

JULIE. Billy! Billy! Where you goin'?

BILLY. Where we goin'?

JIGGER. We're lookin' for the treasure.

JULIE. I don't want you to, Billy. Let me come with you.

JIGGER. No!

JULIE. Billy!

> (*Putting her hands to his chest and feeling the knife.*)

BILLY. I got no time to fool with women. Get out of my way!

(He succeeds in shoving her aside.)

JULIE. Let me have that. Oh, Billy. Please...

(He exits. JIGGER follows. NETTIE puts her arms around JULIE to comfort her. The GIRLS group around them.)

WOMEN.

COMMON SENSE MAY TELL YOU
THAT THE ENDIN' WILL BE SAD,
AND NOW'S THE TIME TO BREAK AND RUN AWAY.
BUT WHAT'S THE USE OF WOND'RIN'
IF THE ENDIN' WILL BE SAD?
HE'S YOUR FELLER AND YOU LOVE HIM –
THERE'S NOTHIN' MORE TO SAY.

(The lights dim and the curtains close.)

[MUSIC NO. 22 "CHANGE OF SCENE (ACT II, SCENE TWO)"]

Scene Two:
Mainland Waterfront, An Hour Later

(Extreme left there is an upright pile, a box, and a bale. At center is a longer bale. Up right center is an assorted heap consisting of a crate, a trunk, a sack and other wharfside oddments.)

(AT RISE: **JIGGER** *is seated on the pile extreme left, smoking.* **BILLY** *is pacing back and forth, right center.)*

BILLY. Suppose he don't come.

JIGGER. He'll come. What will you say to him?

BILLY. I say: "Good evening, sir. Excuse me, sir. Can you tell me the time?" And suppose he answers me. What do I say?

JIGGER. He won't answer you.

> *(***JIGGER*** *throws his knife into the top of the box so that the point sticks and the knife quivers there.)*

BILLY. Have you ever – killed a man before?

JIGGER. If I did, I wouldn't be likely to say so, would I?

BILLY. No, guess you wouldn't. If you did – if tonight we – I mean – suppose some day when *we* die we'll have to come up before – before –

JIGGER. Before who?

BILLY. Well – before God.

JIGGER. You and me? Not a chance!

BILLY. Why not?

JIGGER. What's the highest court they ever dragged you into?

BILLY. Just perlice magistrates, I guess.

JIGGER. Sure. Never been before a Supreme Court judge, have you?

BILLY. No.

JIGGER. Same thing in the next world. For rich folks, the heavenly court and the high judge. For you and me, perlice magistrates. Fer the rich, fine music and chubby little angels –

BILLY. Won't we get any music?

JIGGER. Not a note. All we'll get is justice! There'll be plenty of that for you and me. Yes, sir! Nothin' but justice.

BILLY. It's gettin' late – they'll be comin' back from the clambake. I wish he'd come. Suppose he don't.

JIGGER. He will. What do you say we play some cards while we're waitin'? Time'll pass quicker that way.

BILLY. All right.

JIGGER. Got any money?

BILLY. Eighty cents.

(Crosses to **JIGGER***, sits on small bale, and puts his money on the box.* **JIGGER** *takes out cards and his change.)*

JIGGER. *(Putting money on box and shuffling cards.)* All right, eighty cents. We'll play twenty-one. I'll bank.

(Deals the necessary cards out.)

BILLY. *(Looking at his cards.)* I'll bet the bank.

JIGGER. *(Aloud, to himself.)* Sounds like he's got an ace.

BILLY. I'll take another.

*(***JIGGER** *deals another card to* **BILLY.***)*

Come again!

(JIGGER deals a fourth card.)

Over!

(Throws cards down. JIGGER gathers in the money. BILLY rises, crosses right center, looks off right.)

Wish old sideburns would come and have it over with.

JIGGER. He's a little late.

(Looking up at BILLY.)

Don't you want to go on with the game?

BILLY. Ain't got any more money. I told you.

JIGGER. Want to play on credit?

BILLY. You mean you'll trust me?

JIGGER. No – but I'll deduct it.

BILLY. From what?

JIGGER. From your share of the money. If you win, you deduct it from my share.

BILLY. *(Crossing and sitting on bale.)* All right. Can't wait here doin' nothin'. Drive a feller crazy. How much is the bank?

JIGGER. Sideburns'll have three thousand on him. That's what he always brings the captain. Tonight the captain don't get it. We get it. Fifteen hundred to you. Fifteen hundred to me.

BILLY. Go ahead and deal.

(JIGGER deals.)

Fifty dollars.

(Looks at his card.)

No, a hundred dollars.

>   (**JIGGER** *gives him a card.*)

Enough.

JIGGER. *(Laying down stack and looking at his own cards.)* Twenty-one.

BILLY. All right! This time double or nothin'!

JIGGER. *(Dealing.)* Double or nothin' it is.

BILLY. *(Looking at cards.)* Enough.

JIGGER. *(Laying down his cards.)* Twenty-one.

BILLY. Hey – are you cheatin'?

JIGGER. *(So innocent.)* Me? Do I look like a cheat?

BILLY. (**BILLY** *raps the box impatiently.* **JIGGER** *deals.)* Five hundred!

JIGGER. Dollars?

BILLY. Dollars.

JIGGER. Say, you're a plunger, ain't you? Yes, sir.

BILLY. *(Getting a card.)* Another.

>   (*He gets it.*)

Too much.

JIGGER. That makes seven hundred you owe me.

BILLY. Seven hundred! Double or nothin'.

>   (**JIGGER** *deals.*)

I'll stand pat!

JIGGER. *(Laying down his cards in pretended amazement.)* Twenty-one! A natural!

BILLY. *(Rising and taking hold of* **JIGGER** *by the coat lapels.)* You – you – damn you, you're a dirty crook! You –

(BASCOMBE enters from left. JIGGER coughs, warning BILLY, and then nudges BILLY into action as BASCOMBE crosses to right center. JIGGER runs behind crates. BILLY addresses BASCOMBE.)

Excuse me, sir. Can you tell me the time?

(BASCOMBE turns to BILLY and JIGGER leaps out from behind the crates and tries to stab BASCOMBE. BASCOMBE gets hold of JIGGER's knife hand and twists his wrist, forcing him into a helpless position. BASCOMBE takes his gun from its holster with his free hand, holding BILLY off.)

BASCOMBE. Now don't budge, either one of you. *(To JIGGER.)* Drop that knife.

(JIGGER drops the knife.)

Ahoy, up there on the *Nancy B*! Captain Watson! Anybody up there?

CAPTAIN. *(Offstage.)* Ahoy, down there!

(JIGGER twists himself loose and runs off right. A SAILOR enters from left. BASCOMBE turns and fires a shot at JIGGER as he runs, then turns, holding BILLY off, as the SAILOR gets to BASCOMBE.)

BASCOMBE. *(To the SAILOR.)* Go after that one. He's runnin' up Maple Street. I'll cover the other one.

(The SAILOR runs off after JIGGER.)

There's another bullet in here. Don't forget that – you. Look behind you! What do you see comin'?

BILLY. *(Slowly turning and looking off left.)* Two perlicemen.

BASCOMBE. You wanted to know what time it was. I'll tell you – the time for you will be ten or twenty years in prison.

*(The **TWO POLICEMEN** enter from left.)*

BILLY. Oh, no it won't.

(He clambers up on the pile with his knife drawn.)

BASCOMBE. *(Jeering and covering him with his pistol.)* Where do you think you're escapin' to – the sky?

BILLY. They won't put me in no prison.

(He raises the knife high in the air.)

POLICEMAN. Stop him!

BILLY. *(Stabbing himself in the stomach.)* Julie!

*(He topples off the pile of crates, falling behind them. The **TWO POLICEMEN**, who have made a vain attempt to stop him, rush behind the crates where they proceed to remove his coat, which is later to be used for his pillow. The **CAPTAIN** and another **SAILOR** come on the run from left. The **CAPTAIN** is carrying a lantern, which he puts on the pile, right center.)*

CAPTAIN. *(To **BASCOMBE**.)* How about you, Mr. Bascombe? You all right?

BASCOMBE. Yes, I'm all right. Lucky, though. Very lucky. This is the first time I ever took a pistol with me.

CAPTAIN. *(Looking over crates at **BILLY**.)* Is he dead?

1ST POLICEMAN. I don't think so, he's still breathing.

CAPTAIN. Bring him out here where we can lay him out flat.

(The **CAPTAIN** *looks around to see what can be used for a bed for* **BILLY**. *He spots the bales, crosses to left, and puts the smaller end to end with the larger one center. The* **TWO POLICEMEN** *and the* **SAILOR** *carry* **BILLY** *out and lay him on the bales. The* **CAPTAIN** *speaks to the* **SAILOR** .)*

You go for a doctor. *(To the* **POLICEMAN** *who is holding* **BILLY**'s *coat.)* Put that under his head.

(The **POLICEMAN** *does this. When* **BILLY** *is set, the* **TWO POLICEMEN** *rise; one stands left end of bale, the other right end.)*

BASCOMBE. The fools – the silly fools. They didn't even notice I was comin' from the ship, not to it.

(The **CAPTAIN** *is covering* **BILLY** *with a tarpaulin he found on the top of crates at right center.)*

CAPTAIN. The money they tried to kill for is locked up in my desk!

*(***VOICES** *off left are heard to be singing "June is Bustin' Out All Over," very softly, as if in the distance.)*

BASCOMBE. The fools.

1ST SAILOR. *(The one who chased* **JIGGER**, *returning.)* He got away.

BASCOMBE. *(Hearing the offstage singing as it has become louder.)* What's that?

CAPTAIN. The folk comin' back from the clambake.

(The **PEOPLE** *enter left.)*

BASCOMBE. *(To the* **POLICEMAN**.)* You'd better stop them.

*(***BASCOMBE** *exits.)*

POLICEMAN. Yes, sir.

> *(They cross over and stop the crowd from
> reaching **BILLY**, but one or two get through
> and see the tragedy, and they recognize **BILLY**.
> The **POLICEMAN** gets to these and speaks. The
> singing stops.)*

Get back there. Stand back.

> *(**VOICES** are heard from behind the crowd.)*

1ST VOICE. Who is it?

2ND VOICE. Billy.

3RD VOICE. Billy Bigelow.

4TH VOICE. Poor Julie.

> *(The crowd opens up for **JULIE**, who goes
> straight to **BILLY**, up behind the bales. **NETTIE**
> and the **POLICEMEN** hurry the crowd off
> quietly. They exit left. The **CAPTAIN** remains
> on right of the crates looking upstage. The
> **POLICEMEN** and **NETTIE** also remain.)*

JULIE. *(As she is crossing to him.)* Billy –

BILLY. Little Julie – somethin' I want to tell you –

> *(Pause.)*

I couldn't see anythin' ahead, and Jigger told me how
we could get a hold of a lot of money – and maybe sail
to San Francisco. See?

JULIE. Yes.

BILLY. Tell the baby, if you want, say I had this idea about
San Francisco.

> *(His voice grows weaker.)*

Julie –

JULIE. Yes.

BILLY. Hold my hand tight.

JULIE. I am holdin' it tight – all the time.

BILLY. Tighter – still tighter!

> *(Pause.)*

Julie!

JULIE. Good-by.

> *(He sinks back. **JULIE** kisses his hand. The **CAPTAIN** crosses over, picks **JULIE** up gently. He then bends down and inspects **BILLY**. He rises, looks at **JULIE**.)*

CAPTAIN. The good Lord will help him now, ma'am.

> *(**CARRIE** enters, followed by **ENOCH**. They cross to **JULIE**'s left.)*

CARRIE. Julie – don't be mad at me for sayin' it – but you're better off this way.

ENOCH. Carrie's right.

CARRIE. Julie, tell me, am I right?

JULIE. You're right, Carrie.

CARRIE. *(Looking down at **BILLY**.)* He's better off too, poor feller. Believe me, Julie, he's better off too.

> *(She embraces **JULIE**, weeping.)*

JULIE. Don't cry, Carrie.

CARRIE. God be with you, Julie.

> *(**JULIE** smiles at her wearily. **ENOCH** takes **CARRIE** by the arm and leads her off down left. We hear **VOICES** off left.)*

MRS. MULLIN. *(Offstage.)* Where is he? No, no, please.

> (MRS. MULLIN *comes in on the run from left,*
> *followed by two* GIRLS, *who try to stop her.*)

GIRL. Don't let her!

> (MRS. MULLIN *stops left center, looks at* BILLY,
> *then at* JULIE *questioningly.* JULIE *steps*
> *back – a silent invitation to come and pass*
> *in front of her.* MRS. MULLIN *walks slowly to*
> *where* BILLY *lies. After a moment she brushes*
> BILLY's *hair off his forehead, as she used to do.*
> *Then* NETTIE, *the* POLICEMEN *and all exit,*
> *leaving only* JULIE *and* MRS. MULLIN *on the*
> *stage with* BILLY. MRS. MULLIN *gets up and*
> *turns slowly to look at* JULIE, *who looks back*
> *at her.* MRS. MULLIN *tries a faint little smile,*
> *then turns and exits left.* JULIE *returns to*
> BILLY, *leans over, and restores the stray lock*
> *to where it was before* MRS. MULLIN *took the*
> *liberty to brush it back.*)

JULIE. Sleep, Billy – sleep. Sleep peaceful, like a good boy.
I knew why you hit me. You were quick-tempered and
unhappy. I always knew everythin' you were thinkin'.
But you didn't always know what I was thinkin'. One
thing I never told you – skeered you'd laugh at me. I'll
tell you now –

> (*Even now she has to make an effort to*
> *overcome her shyness in saying it.*)

I love you. I love you. (*In a whisper.*) I love – you.

(*Smiles.*) I was always ashamed to say it out loud. But
now I said it. Didn't I?

> (*She takes the shawl off her shoulders and*
> *drapes it over* BILLY. NETTIE *comes in from*
> *left.* JULIE *looks up and sees her, lets out a cry,*
> *and runs to her.*)

What am I goin' to do?

NETTIE. Do? Why, you gotta stay on here with me – so's I ken be with you when you hev the baby.

> (JULIE *buries her head in* NETTIE's *shoulder and holds tightly to her.*)

Main thing is to keep on *livin'* – keep on *keerin'* what's goin' to happen. 'Member that sampler you gave me? 'Member what it says?

JULIE. The words? Sure. Used to sing 'em in school.

NETTIE. Sing 'em now – see if you know what they mean.

[MUSIC NO. 23 "YOU'LL NEVER WALK ALONE"]

JULIE.
WHEN YOU WALK THROUGH A STORM
KEEP YOUR CHIN UP HIGH,
AND DON'T BE AFRAID OF THE...

> (JULIE *breaks off, sobbing.* NETTIE *starts the song over again.*)

NETTIE.
WHEN YOU WALK THROUGH A STORM
KEEP YOUR CHIN UP HIGH,
AND DON'T BE AFRAID OF THE DARK.
AT THE END OF THE STORM
IS A GOLDEN SKY
AND THE SWEET, SILVER SONG OF A LARK.
WALK ON THROUGH THE WIND,
WALK ON THROUGH THE RAIN,
THOUGH YOUR DREAMS BE TOSSED AND BLOWN.
WALK ON, WALK ON, WITH HOPE IN YOUR HEART,
AND YOU'LL NEVER WALK ALONE!
YOU'LL NEVER WALK ALONE.

[MUSIC NO. 24 "INCIDENTAL"]

(JULIE *and* NETTIE *kneel in prayer. The* TWO
HEAVENLY FRIENDS *enter from right and
cross to* BILLY. *The chorus hums through the
rest of the scene from offstage.*)

1ST HEAVENLY FRIEND. Get up, Billy.

BILLY. Huh?

1ST HEAVENLY FRIEND. Get up.

BILLY. *(Straightening up.)* Who are you?

2ND HEAVENLY FRIEND. Shake yourself up. Got to get
goin'.

BILLY. *(Looking up at them and turning front, still sitting.)*
Goin'? Where?

1ST HEAVENLY FRIEND. Never mind where. Important
thing is you can't stay here.

BILLY. *(Turning left, looks at* JULIE.*)* Julie!

(*The lights dim, and a cloud gauze drop
comes in behind* BILLY *and the* HEAVENLY
FRIENDS.*)*

1ST HEAVENLY FRIEND. She can't hear you.

BILLY. Who decided that?

1ST HEAVENLY FRIEND. You did. When you killed yourself.

BILLY. I see! So it's over!

1ST HEAVENLY FRIEND. It isn't as simple as that. As long as
there is one person on earth who remembers you – it
isn't over.

BILLY. What're you goin' to do to me?

1ST HEAVENLY FRIEND. We weren't going to do anything.
We jest came down to fetch you – take you up to the
jedge.

BILLY. Judge! Am I goin' before the Lord God Himself?

1ST HEAVENLY FRIEND. What hev you ever done thet you should come before Him?

BILLY. *(His anger rising.)* So that's it. Just like Jigger said – "No Supreme Court for little people – just perlice magistrates!"

1ST HEAVENLY FRIEND. Who said anythin' about...?

BILLY. I tell you, if they kick me around up there like they did on earth, I'm goin' to do somethin' about it! I'm dead and I got nothin' to lose. I'm goin' to stand up for my rights! I tell you, I'm goin' before the Lord God Himself – straight to the top! Y'hear?

1ST HEAVENLY FRIEND. Simmer down, Billy. Simmer down.

[MUSIC NO. 25 "THE HIGHEST JUDGE OF ALL"]

BILLY.

TAKE ME BEYOND THE PEARLY GATES,
THROUGH A BEAUTIFUL MARBLE HALL,
TAKE ME BEFORE THE HIGHEST THRONE
AND LET ME JUDGED BY THE HIGHEST JUDGE OF ALL!

LET THE LORD SHOUT AND YELL,
LET HIS EYES FLASH FLAME,
I PROMISE NOT TO QUIVER WHEN HE CALLS MY NAME;
LET HIM SEND ME TO HELL,
BUT BEFORE I GO,
I FEEL THAT I'M ENTITLED TO A HELL OF A SHOW!

WANT PINK-FACED ANGELS ON A PURPLE CLOUD,
TWANGIN' ON THEIR HARPS TILL THEIR FINGERS GET
    RED.
WANT ORGAN MUSIC – LET IT ROLL OUT LOUD,
ROLLIN' LIKE A WAVE WASHIN' OVER MY HEAD!
WANT EV'RY STAR IN HEAVEN
HANGIN' IN THE ROOM,
SHININ' IN MY EYES

WHEN I HEAR MY DOOM!

RECKON MY SINS ARE GOOD, BIG SINS,
AND THE PUNISHMENT WON'T BE SMALL.
SO TAKE ME BEFORE THE HIGHEST THRONE
AND LET ME BE JUDGED BY THE HIGHEST JUDGE OF ALL!

(**1ST HEAVENLY FRIEND** *gestures to* **BILLY** *to follow. They exit.*)

[MUSIC NO. 26 "EXIT OF BILLY AND HEAVENLY FRIENDS (CHANGE OF SCENE)"]

Scene Three:
Up There

(A celestial clothesline is seen stretching back through infinity, but one portion of it is strung across as far downstage as possible. There is a celestial stepladder standing right center upstage of the line. It resembles our own stepladders except that it shimmers with a silvery light. The clothesline is quite full of shimmering stars. There is a basket full of stars on the shelf behind the ladder.)

*(AT RISE: The **STARKEEPER** is seated on the top of the stepladder, and as the lights come up, he can be seen hanging out stars and dusting them with a silver-handled white feather duster.)*

*(**BILLY** and the **TWO HEAVENLY FRIENDS** are seen making their way through the clouds from stage left to right, emerging a moment later through entrance down right into the back yard. The **1ST HEAVENLY FRIEND** enters. He stops, stage right center, faces front, and speaks.)*

1ST HEAVENLY FRIEND. Billy!

BILLY. *(Entering.)* Hey, what is this!

*(Crossing and speaking to **STARKEEPER**.)*

Who are you?

STARKEEPER. Never mind who I am, Bigelow.

BILLY. *(To **FRIEND**.)* Where am I?

STARKEEPER. *(Although question was not addressed to him.)* You're in the back yard of heaven.

(Pointing off right.)

There's the gates over there.

BILLY. The pearly gates!

STARKEEPER. Nope. The pearly gates are in front. Those are the back gates. They're just mother-of-pearly.

BILLY. I don't wanta go in no back gate. I wanta go before the highest –

STARKEEPER. You'll go where we send you, young man.

BILLY. Now look here!

STARKEEPER. Don't yell.

BILLY. I didn't yell.

STARKEEPER. Well, don't.

(He takes a star off the line.)

(To 1ST **HEAVENLY FRIEND.***)* This one's finished. Brother Joshua, please hang it over Salem, Mass.

1ST HEAVENLY FRIEND. *(Crossing over and taking star.)* Ay-ah.

(Exits off left.)

STARKEEPER. *(Taking a notebook out of his pocket.)* Now, this is a routine question I gotta ask everybody. Is there anythin' on earth you left unfinished? The reason I ask you is you're entitled to go back fer one day – if you want to.

BILLY. I don't know. *(Doggedly.)* Guess as long as I'm here, I won't go back.

STARKEEPER. *(Jotting down in a notebook.)* "Waives his right to go back."

BILLY. Can I ask you somethin'? I'd like to know if the baby will be a boy or a girl.

STARKEEPER. We'll come to that later.

BILLY. But I'm only askin' –

STARKEEPER. Jest let me do the askin' – you do the answerin'. I got my orders. You left yer wife hevin' thet baby comin' – with nothin' fer 'em to live on. Why'd you do thet?

BILLY. I couldn't get work and I couldn't bear to see her –

(*Pause.*)

STARKEEPER. You couldn't bear to see her cry. Why not come right out and say it? Why are you afraid of sayin' the right word? Why are you ashamed you loved Julie?

BILLY. I ain't ashamed of anything.

STARKEEPER. Why'd you beat her?

BILLY. I didn't beat her – I wouldn't beat a little thing like that – I hit her.

STARKEEPER. Why?

BILLY. Well, y'see we'd argue. And she'd say this and I'd say that – and she'd be right – so I hit her.

STARKEEPER. Hmm! Are you sorry you hit her?

BILLY. Ain't sorry for anythin'.

STARKEEPER. (*Taking his basket coming down off the ladder.*) You ken be as sot and pernicketty as you want. Up here patience is as endless as time. We ken wait.

(*He turns to* **BILLY** *in a more friendly way.*)

Now look here, son, it's only fair to tell you – you're in a pretty tight corner. Fact is you haven't done enough good in yer life to get in there – not even through the back door.

BILLY. (*Turning away.*) All right. If I can't get in – I can't.

STARKEEPER. *(Testily.)* I didn't say you can't. Said you ain't done enough so *far*. You might still make it – if you tried hard enough.

BILLY. How?

STARKEEPER. Why don't you go down to earth fer a day like I said you could? Do somethin' real fine fer someone.

BILLY. Aw – what could I do?

STARKEEPER. Well, fer one thing you might do yer little daughter some good.

BILLY. *(Turning to* **STARKEEPER**, *elated.)* A daughter! It's a girl – my baby!

STARKEEPER. Ain't a baby any more. She's fifteen years old.

BILLY. How could that be? I just come from there.

STARKEEPER. You got to get used to a new way of tellin' time, Billy. A year on earth is just a minute up here. Would you like to look down and see her?

BILLY. Could I? Could I see her from here?

STARKEEPER. Sure could. Follow me.

> *(***STARKEEPER** *and* **BILLY** *cross down right. The lights dim and the gauze cloud curtain descends behind them.)*

BILLY. Tell me – is she happy?

STARKEEPER. No, she ain't, Billy. She's a lot like you. That's why I figure you're the one could help her most – if you was there.

BILLY. If she ain't happy, I don't want to look.

STARKEEPER. *(Looking off left, as if toward the earth.)* Well, right this minute she appears to be hevin' a fine time. Yes, sir! There she is runnin' on the beach. Got her shoes and stockin's off.

BILLY. Like I used to do!

STARKEEPER. Don't you think you better take a look?

BILLY. Where is she? What do I have to do to see her?

(The music begins.)

[MUSIC NO. 27 "BALLET"]

STARKEEPER. Jest look and wait. The power to see her will come to you.

(He puts his hand lightly on BILLY's shoulder.)

BILLY. Is that her? Little kid with tangled hair?

(The lights dim. The curtain goes up on a dark stage.)

(As the lights on BILLY and the STARKEEPER are dimming, a spotlight comes up on LOUISE, arms outstretched.)

STARKEEPER. Pretty – ain't she?

BILLY. My little girl!

(BILLY and the STARKEEPER back off down right and the entire stage is suddenly flooded with light.)

Scene Four:
Down Here On A Beach, Fifteen Years Later

(AT RISE: We see **LOUISE** *standing alone, upstage center. As soon as the lights come up, the music of "If I Loved You" begins [measure 9], and she can be seen running and jumping joyously in her bare feet. [Measure 43] She turns a somersault and lies down on the sand to stare at the sky. [Measure 47] Two* **RUFFIANS** *come leap-frogging in, and* **LOUISE** *joins them in their rough play. Presently* **ENOCH SNOW** *enters from up right [measure 98], leading his six very well-behaved* **CHILDREN***, all wearing their Sunday hats. They cross to downstage left, forming a diagonal line from down left to up center. [Measure 106] They stop in amazement to see the boisterous rough-housing of* **LOUISE** *and her* **COMPANIONS** – **ENOCH SNOW** *strongly disapproves.* **LOUISE** *tries to make friends with them and invites them to join in her play [measure 136], but, taking their cue from their father's horrified face, they just stand there shaking their heads. She finally gets the attention of two of them, who step out of line and laugh heartily at the antics of* **LOUISE***, but* **SNOW** *stands there sternly and watches them. They feel his glare, look up at him and step meekly back into line. They snub her and finally exit [measure 148], led by* **SNOW***, but as they go, one of them, [measure 160] a curious* **LITTLE MISS STUCK UP***, steps out of line and lags behind the rest. She examines* **LOUISE***'s poor dress and bare feet with unfriendly dislike, circling around her and stopping on her left [measure 187].)*

ENOCH'S DAUGHTER. *(Boastfully.)* My father bought me *my* pretty dress.

LOUISE. My father would've bought me a pretty dress, too. He was a barker on a carousel.

ENOCH'S DAUGHTER. Your father was a *thief!*

(They stand there just looking at each other. Finally **ENOCH'S DAUGHTER** *tries to sneak away. She starts slowly circling counterclockwise.* **LOUISE** *follows her, their pace increasing as the circle gets bigger until she chases* **ENOCH'S DAUGHTER** *off left. When* **LOUISE** *returns [measure 188] she is wearing the big new hat that* **ENOCH'S DAUGHTER** *was wearing. She ties the bow, and then, imitating something she has seen proper ladies do, licks her fingers [measure 192] and smoothes back the upsweep of her hair [measure 193]. Then she flips her skirt [measure 194].* **LOUISE** *and the two* **RUFFIANS** *laugh.)*

(They get ready for another game of leap frog when a **CARNIVAL TROUPE** *is seen entering upstage right [measure 196].* **LOUISE** *is entranced. One* **YOUNG MAN**, *the leader of the Troupe, is the type* **LOUISE** *believes her father to have been when he was young. He enters with a* **GIRL ACROBAT** *on his shoulder. She is holding a parasol. The* **YOUNG MAN** *sets her down. [Measure 212] She places her parasol in the center of the stage. The* **CARNIVAL TROUPE** *gets into position and [at measure 220] begins to dance around the parasol, as if they were horses on a carousel. At the same time* **LOUISE**, *drawn to the parasol, picks it up and begins to revolve with the* **CARNIVAL TROUPE**. *As they perform a brutal and frenetic waltz,* **LOUISE** *becomes frightened,*

crouches down and runs out of the circle. The
ACROBAT *approaches one of the* **RUFFIANS**
(downstage right) and playfully ruffles his
hair. This scares him, and he dashes off right
[measure 244].)

(At the same time the **YOUNG MAN** *notices*
LOUISE *and goes to shake her hand [measure*
248]. Then they rejoin the dancing
CARNIVAL TROUPE. *[At measure 292] The*
ACROBAT *sees* **LOUISE** *holding the stolen*
parasol and demands it back. **LOUISE** *gives*
her the parasol. [Measure 296] The **YOUNG**
MAN *and* **LOUISE** *meet face to face. He tells*
her not to mind and winks at her. As the
ACROBAT *checks her parasol for any damage,*
LOUISE*, fascinated by the glittery piece of*
silk decorating the **ACROBAT**'s *skirt, touches*
it. [Measure 302] The **ACROBAT***, annoyed,*
pulls away from **LOUISE.** *[Measure 316]*
However, the **YOUNG MAN** *snatches the*
scarf from the **ACROBAT**'s *skirt and gives*
it to **LOUISE.** *The* **CARNIVAL TROUPE** *begin*
their exit upstage right [by measure 320].
LOUISE *remains alone on the beach, dancing*
dreamily with the scarf. [Measure 338] The
YOUNG MAN*, who has waited behind, watches*
her. She becomes aware of his presence, and
awkwardly approaches him. [Measure 360]
Together they dance a pas-de-deux. [Measure
416] Eventually he grows frightened of her
intensity. Realizing how young and innocent
she is, he reluctantly leaves her. [Measure
428] **LOUISE** *feels humiliated and ashamed.*
She weeps.)

([Measure 436] The **SNOW CHILDREN**
re-enter from upstage left, dancing a
Polonaise. [Measure 454] **LOUISE** *tries to join*

them but is constantly pushed out. [Measure 486] **LOUISE** *pretends she doesn't care and dances by herself, but her heart is breaking. [Measure 502]* **MISS SNOW** *makes fun of her, all the* **CHILDREN** *begin to mock her, until she turns on them in desperation [measure 508]. They are frozen with awe and fear as she speaks to them in a voice filled with deep injury and the fury of a hopeless outcast.)*

LOUISE. *(Whispers.)* I hate you – I hate all of you!

(The **CHILDREN** *back away and then begin dancing again [measure 515].* **LOUISE** *stands there looking at them, heartbroken and alone, as the gauze cloud curtain falls. We see* **BILLY** *and the* **STARKEEPER**, *who have been watching all of this from "up there," back in their original positions.)*

[MUSIC NO. 28 "MY LITTLE GIRL – MUSIC UNDER SCENE "]

BILLY. Why did you make me look?

STARKEEPER. You said you wanted to.

BILLY. I know what she's goin' through.

STARKEEPER. Somethin' like what happened to you when you was a kid, ain't it?

BILLY. Somebody ought to help her.

STARKEEPER. Ay-ah. Somebody ought to. You ken go down any time. Offer's still open.

(The **1ST HEAVENLY FRIEND** *enters to guide* **BILLY** *if he wants to go.* **BILLY** *starts toward him; then, getting a sudden idea, he turns back and stealthily takes a star from the* **STARKEEPER**'s *basket. Both the* **STARKEEPER**

and the **1ST HEAVENLY FRIEND** *are aware of this, but pretend not to notice.* **BILLY** *waves an elaborate good-by to the* **STARKEEPER** *and, whistling casually to quell suspicion, he starts away with the* **1ST HEAVENLY FRIEND.***)*

Scene Five:
Outside Julie's Cottage

*(AT RISE: **JULIE** and **CARRIE** are seated outside the cottage, having coffee.)*

CARRIE. *(Seated left of **JULIE**, continuing a narrative.)* ...And so the next day we all climbed to the top of the Statue of Liberty – Enoch and me and the nine kids.

JULIE. Did you go to any theayters in New York?

CARRIE. 'Course we did!

JULIE. Did you see any of them there "extravaganzas"?

CARRIE. Enoch took me to one of them things. The curtain went up an' the fust thing y'see is twelve hussies with nothin' on their legs but tights!

JULIE. What happened then?

CARRIE. Well! Enoch jest grabbed hold o' my arm and dragged me out of the theayter! But I went back the next day – to a matinee – to see how the story come out.

JULIE. All by yerself?

*(**CARRIE** nods.)*

Lucky you didn't see anybody you know.

CARRIE. I did.

JULIE. Who?

CARRIE. Enoch!

*(**JULIE** clasps her hand over her mouth to keep from laughing. Then she gets the cups together. **CARRIE** gets up.)*

(Animatedly.) There was one girl who sung an awful ketchy song.

(She walks to the back of her chair. **LOUISE** *enters from the house, unnnoticed.)*

She threw her leg over a fence like this –

(As she is swinging her leg over the chair, she sees **LOUISE** *and hastily puts her leg down.)*

– and it rained all day!

*(***JULIE***, her back toward* **LOUISE***, stares at* **CARRIE** *in wonder. She gathers that something is up, turns right, and sees* **LOUISE***.)*

JULIE. Oh-h-h. Louise, take these cups into the kitchen, dear. That's a good girl.

*(***LOUISE*** *takes the cups into the house.)*

CARRIE. She threw her leg over a fence like this –

(She swings her leg over the chair and pulls her skirt up over her knee.)

and she sung –

[MUSIC NO. 29 "CARRIE'S INCIDENTAL"]

(Unaccompanied.)

I'M A TOMBOY, JEST A TOMBOY!
I'M A MADCAP MAIDEN FROM BROADWAY!

*(***ENOCH*** *enters followed by their eldest son,* **ENOCH, JR.***, but* **CARRIE** *does not see them.* **JULIE** *tries to warn her.)*

I'M A TOMBOY, A MERRY TOMBOY!
I'M A MADCAP MAIDEN FROM BROADWAY!

ENOCH. *(Taking his son by the shoulders.)* Turn yer eyes away, Junior!

(Turns his **SON***'s face away.)*

CARRIE. *(Taking her leg off the chair and standing there guiltily.)* I was jest tellin' Julie about thet show – *Madcap Maidens.*

ENOCH. We also saw *Julius Caesar.* Wouldn't thet be a better play to quote from?

CARRIE. I don't remember much of thet one. All the men was dressed in nightgowns and it made me sleepy.

JULIE. *(Trying to change the subject.)* Won't you set down and visit with us?

ENOCH. Afeared we hevn't time. Mrs. Snow and I hev to stop at the minister's on our way to the graduation. *(To* **CARRIE.***)* And I'll thank you not to sing "I'm a Tomboy" to the minister's wife.

CARRIE. I already did.

ENOCH. *(Giving his* **SON** *a good slap on the back.)* Come, Junior!

> *(***LOUISE** *comes out of the house just as* **JUNIOR** *turns to his father.* **JUNIOR** *sees* **LOUISE** *and gets a new idea.)*

ENOCH, JR. Pa, ken I stay and talk to Louise?

> *(***ENOCH** *looks stern.* **CARRIE** *crosses to* **ENOCH.***)*

Jest for five minutes.

ENOCH. No!

CARRIE. *(Slapping* **ENOCH***'s back in the same manner as* **ENOCH** *slapped* **JUNIOR.***)* Aw, let him!

ENOCH. All right. Five minutes. No more.

JULIE. *(Going into house.)* Good-by.

CARRIE. See you at the graduation.

> *(***JULIE** *exits into house.)*

ENOCH. *(Taking* **CARRIE** *to exit.)* Still lallygaggin'. You'd think a woman with nine children'd hev more sense.

CARRIE. If I hed more sense I wouldn't hev nine children!

> *(She crosses in front of* **ENOCH** *and exits. He follows.)*

LOUISE. I wish I could go to New York.

ENOCH, JR. What are you goin' to do after you graduate?

LOUISE. *(Lowering her voice, as* **BILLY** *and* **FRIEND** *enter left.)* Listen, Enoch – ken you keep a secret?

> *(***JUNIOR** *solemnly crosses his heart and spits.)*

BILLY. *(To* **HEAVENLY FRIEND.***)* Can she see me?

1ST HEAVENLY FRIEND. Only if you want her to.

> *(They remain silent observers of the scene,* **BILLY** *standing by the trellis,* **1ST HEAVENLY FRIEND** *extreme downstage left.)*

ENOCH, JR. Well, what's the secret?

LOUISE. I'm goin' to be an actress. There's a Troupe comin' through here next week. I met a feller – says he's the advance man, or somethin' – says he'll help me!

ENOCH, JR. *(Horrified.)* You mean run away?

> *(She puts her fingers to her lips to shush him.* **BILLY** *winces.* **1ST HEAVENLY FRIEND** *watches* **BILLY.***)*

I won't let you do it, Louise.

LOUISE. How'll you stop me?

ENOCH, JR. I'll marry you. That's how. The hardest thing'll be to persuade Papa to let me marry beneath my station.

LOUISE. You needn't bother about marryin' beneath your station! I wouldn't have you. And I wouldn't have that stuck-up buzzard for a father-in-law if you give me a million dollars!

> (BILLY *looks at* 1ST HEAVENLY FRIEND *and smiles, happy over this.*)

ENOCH, JR. *(Outraged, hit in a tender spot.)* You're a fine one to talk about my father! What about yer own? A cheap barker on a carousel – and he beat your mother!

LOUISE. *(Giving* JUNIOR *a good punch.)* You get out of here! You sleeky little la-de-da!

> *(Spins him around and aims a well-directed kick at him.* BILLY, *seeing all this, puts out his foot and trips* JUNIOR *just as he is passing him.)*

I'll – I'll kill you – you –

> *(*JUNIOR, *baffled, runs out left.* LOUISE *suddenly turns, crosses to her chair, sinks on it, and sobs.* BILLY *looks over at* LOUISE, *who is a very heartbroken little girl. He turns to the* 1ST HEAVENLY FRIEND.)*

BILLY. If I want her to see me, she will?

> *(The* 1ST HEAVENLY FRIEND *nods.* BILLY *approaches* LOUISE *timidly.)*

Little girl – Louise!

> *(She looks up through her tears.)*

LOUISE. Who are you?

BILLY. I... I...

> *(He's nearly as rattled as he was the night he suddenly faced* BASCOMBE *on the wharf.)*

LOUISE. How did you know my name?

BILLY. Somebody told me you lived here. I knew your father.

LOUISE. My father!

BILLY. I heard what that little whippersnapper said. It ain't true – any of it.

LOUISE. It is true – all of it.

(*Pause. He is stunned.*)

BILLY. Did your mother tell you that?

LOUISE. No, but every kid in town knows it. They've been throwin' it up at me ever since I ken remember. I wish I was dead.

(*She looks away to hide her tears.*)

BILLY. (*Softly.*) What – what did yer *mother* say about – him?

LOUISE. Oh, she's told me a lot of fairy stories about how he died in San Francisco – and she's always sayin' what a handsome fellow he was –

BILLY. Well, he was!

LOUISE. (*Hopeful, rising.*) Was he – really?

BILLY. He was the handsomest feller around here.

LOUISE. You really knew him, did you? And he was handsome?

(*He nods his head.*)

What else about him? Know anythin' else *good* about him?

BILLY. (*Passing right hand through his hair.*) Well-ll... he used to tell funny jokes at the carousel and make people laugh.

LOUISE. *(Her face lighting up.)* Did he?

(They both laugh.)

What else?

(Pause. He's stuck and changes the subject.)

BILLY. Look – I want to give you a present.

LOUISE. *(Backing up right, immediately suspicious.)* Don't come in, mister. My mother wouldn't like it.

BILLY. I don't mean you any harm, child. I want to give you somethin'.

LOUISE. Don't you come any closer. You go 'way with yer frightful face. You scare me.

BILLY. Don't chase me away. I want to give you a present – somethin' pretty – somethin' wonderful –

(He looks at the 1ST HEAVENLY FRIEND, who turns front and smiles. BILLY takes the star from his inside vest pocket. LOUISE looks at the star with wonderment, then at BILLY.)

LOUISE. What's that?

BILLY. Psst! A star.

(He points up to the sky with right hand to indicate whence it came. LOUISE is terrified now.)

LOUISE. *(Backing up right.)* Go away!

BILLY. *(Growing panicky and taking her arm.)* Darling, please – I want to help you.

LOUISE. *(Trying to pull her arm away.)* Don't call me "darling." Let go of my arm!

BILLY. I want to make you happy. Take this –

LOUISE. No!

BILLY. Please!

> *(She pulls away from him, holding out her right hand to keep him away from her.)*

Please – dear –

> *(Impulsively, involuntarily, he slaps her hand. She is startled.)*

LOUISE. Mother!

> *(She runs into the house.)*

Mother!

> *(BILLY puts the star on the chair nearest center. Then he looks at the 1ST HEAVENLY FRIEND guiltily.)*

1ST HEAVENLY FRIEND. Failure! You struck out blindly again. All you ever do to get out of difficulty – hit someone you love! Failure!

JULIE. *(Coming out of house, agitated.)* Where is he?

[MUSIC NO. 30 "PORCH SCENE (IF I LOVED YOU – REPRISE)"]

> *(She stops suddenly. BILLY turns to her. She stares at him.)*

BILLY. *(To HEAVENLY FRIEND, but looking at JULIE.)* I don't want her to see me.

1ST HEAVENLY FRIEND. Then she doesn't.

BILLY. She looks like she saw me before I said that.

LOUISE. *(Coming out of the house and crossing downstage of BILLY, almost touching him.)* Oh, he's gone! *(Turning to JULIE.)* I didn't make it up, Mother. Honest – there was a strange man here and he hit me – hard – I heard the sound of it – but it didn't hurt, Mother! It didn't hurt at all – it was jest as if he – kissed my hand!

JULIE. Go into the house, child!

LOUISE. What's happened, Mother?

> (**JULIE** *just stares at the same place.*)

Don't you believe me?

JULIE. Yes, I believe you.

LOUISE. (*Coming closer to* **JULIE.**) Then why don't you tell me why you're actin' so funny?

JULIE. It's nothin', darlin'.

LOUISE. But is it possible, Mother, fer someone to hit you hard like that – real loud and hard – and not hurt you at all?

JULIE. It's possible, dear – fer someone to hit you – hit you hard – and not hurt at all.

> (**JULIE** *and* **LOUISE** *embrace and start for the house.* **LOUISE** *exits into house, but* **JULIE** *sees the star that* **BILLY** *had placed on the chair and goes toward it. As she does so, the lights dim slowly. She picks up the star and holds it to her breast.*)

BILLY. Julie – Julie!

> (*She stands transfixed.*)

LONGING TO TELL YOU,
BUT AFRAID AND SHY,
I LET MY GOLDEN CHANCES PASS ME BY.
NOW I'VE LOST YOU;
SOON I WILL GO IN THE MIST OF DAY,
AND YOU NEVER WILL KNOW
HOW I LOVED YOU,
HOW I LOVED YOU.

> (*The lights fade out as* **JULIE** *goes into the house. As* **BILLY** *crosses to the* **1ST HEAVENLY FRIEND,** *the cloud curtain falls behind him.*)

She took the star – she took it! Seems like she knew I was here.

1ST HEAVENLY FRIEND. Julie would always know.

BILLY. She never changes.

1ST HEAVENLY FRIEND. No, Julie never changes.

BILLY. But my little girl – my Louise – I gottta do somethin' fer her.

1ST HEAVENLY FRIEND. So far you haven't done much.

BILLY. I know. I know.

1ST HEAVENLY FRIEND. Time's runnin' out.

BILLY. But it ain't over yet. I want an extension! I gotta see her graduation.

1ST HEAVENLY FRIEND. All right, Billy!

(They exit. The blue lights dim on the curtain. The curtain rises in the dark. The lights flash up on the next scene.)

Scene Six:
Outside A Schoolhouse, The Same Day

(AT RISE: The **GRADUATING CLASS** *sits massed on three rows of benches. The* **GIRLS**, *all dressed alike in white, are seated on the first two benches. The* **BOYS**, *wearing blue serge suits, sit on the third bench. The* **BOYS** *who cannot be seated on the third bench are standing on the steps of the schoolhouse, behind the benches. Stage left is a bench standing at an angle.* **JULIE** *is seated on the downstage end of the bench,* **NETTIE** *is seated alongside of her. There are* **TWO OTHER PERSONS** *on this bench and other relatives of the graduating class are lined up behind it. Stage right, there is a small platform on which is a speakers' stand. Upstage of this stand,* **DR. SELDON** *is seated on a chair.* **MR. BASCOMBE** *is seated on a chair downstage of the stand.* **ENOCH** *and* **CARRIE** *and their entire family are standing downstage right.* **LOUISE** *is seated on the extreme left end of the first bench with the graduating* **GIRLS**. *As the lights come up, the* **PRINCIPAL** *is standing behind the speakers' stand. All are applauding and a* **YOUNG GIRL** *has just received her diploma. She goes up and joins the others.)*

PRINCIPAL. Enoch Snow, Junior!

*(***ENOCH, JR.** *comes up. His applause is led by his not inconsiderable family –* **ENOCH, SR.**, **CARRIE** *and his* **BROTHERS** *and* **SISTERS**. *They form a solid cheering section. As* **ENOCH, JR.** *returns to his place, one of his* **SISTERS** *sitting in the first row puts out her foot and trips him. He looks around, and she applauds vigorously. He walks on.)*

BABY SISTER. Yah!

> (**CARRIE** *pulls her back in line with the rest of the family.*)

PRINCIPAL. Miss Louise Bigelow.

> (**JULIE** *steps out and applauds.* **CARRIE** *claps her hands a few times, and there is not much more.* **LOUISE** *walks up, receives her diploma sullenly, and joins the group again.* **BILLY** *and the* **1ST HEAVENLY FRIEND** *have come in, down right, in time to see this.*)

Our speaker this year is the most popular, best-loved man in our town – Dr. Seldon.

> (*The* **PRINCIPAL** *steps down from the speakers' stand and stands behind* **MR. BASCOMBE.** **DR. SELDON** *now takes his place on the stand. He adjusts his spectacles, and as he does so,* **BILLY** *speaks to the* **1ST HEAVENLY FRIEND.**)

BILLY. Say! He reminds me of that feller up on the ladder.

1ST HEAVENLY FRIEND. Yes, a lot of these country doctors and ministers remind you of him.

DOCTOR SELDON. It's the custom at these graduations to pick out some old duck like me to preach at the kids.

> (*Laughter.*)

I can't preach to you. Know you all too well. Brought most of you into the world. Rubbed liniment on yer backs, poured castor oil down yer throats.

> (*A shudder runs through them, and a* **GIRL** *laughs. All look at her and she is mortified.*)

Well, all I hope is that now I got you this far, you'll turn out to be worth all the trouble I took with you!

(He pauses, looks steadily at them, his voice more earnest.)

I can't tell you any sure way to happiness. All I know is you got to go out and find it fer yourselves.

(BILLY goes over to LOUISE.)

You can't lean on the success of your parents. That's their success. *(Directing his words to LOUISE.)* And don't be held back by their failures! Makes no difference what they did or didn't do. You jest stand on yer own two feet.

BILLY. *(To LOUISE.)* Listen to him. Believe him.

(She looks up suddenly.)

DOCTOR SELDON. The world belongs to you as much as to the next feller. Don't give up! And try not to be skeered o' people not likin' you – jest you try likin' *them*. Jest keep yer faith and courage, and you'll come out all right. It's like what we used to sing every mornin' when I went to school. Mebbe you still sing it – I dunno.

[MUSIC NO. 31 "FINALE ULTIMO (YOU'LL NEVER WALK ALONE – REPRISE)"]

(He recites.) "When you walk through a storm keep yer chin up high..." *(To the KIDS.)* Know thet one?

(They nod eagerly, stand and go on with the song.)

ALL. *(Very quietly.)*
AND DON'T BE AFRAID OF THE DARK.

BILLY. *(To LOUISE.)* Believe him, darling! Believe.

(LOUISE stands, joining the others, who are standing as they sing. NOTE: At this point everyone on stage is standing except for JULIE.)

ALL.

AT THE END OF THE STORM
IS A GOLDEN SKY,
AND THE SWEET, SILVER SONG OF A LARK.

> *(BILLY crosses back of bench left and stands behind JULIE, who is now the only person sitting.)*

WALK ON THROUGH THE WIND,
WALK ON THROUGH THE RAIN,
THOUGH YOUR DREAMS BE TOSSED AND BLOWN.

BILLY. *(To JULIE.)* I loved you, Julie. Know that I loved you!

> *(JULIE's face lights up, she stands as she starts singing with the rest.)*

ALL (WITH JULIE).

WALK ON, WALK ON, WITH HOPE IN YOUR HEART,
AND YOU'LL NEVER WALK ALONE!

> *(LOUISE moves in closer to the group. Tentatively, she puts her arm around the GIRL to her right. Responding, the GIRL turns to LOUISE and smiles. LOUISE's eyes shine. The 1ST HEAVENLY FRIEND smiles and beckons BILLY to follow him. BILLY does. As they pass the DOCTOR, he watches and smiles wisely.)*

YOU'LL NEVER WALK ALONE.

The Curtain Falls

[MUSIC NO. 32 "EXIT MUSIC"]